Murder in Aisle Three

An Alton Oaks Mystery

by

Megan Rivers

For information, email **Cozy Cat Press**, cozycatpress@aol.com or visit our website at: www.cozycatpress.com

COZY CAT
P R E S S

ISBN: 978-1-946063-24-3

Printed in the United States of America

Cover design by Paula Ellenberger
www.paulaellenberger.com

1 2 3 4 5 6 7 8 9 10

To my hometown of Evergreen Park, for my roots...
and for being the positive change I needed, then and
now.

PROLOGUE

"That'll be eight sixty-seven," Sara said, pulling her dyed blonde hair behind her ear and forcing a smile at Mr. Deering. He had just spent the better part of an hour collecting a variety of canned fruits and a tub of cottage cheese at the store where Sara had worked since she was sixteen.

Sara only half-listened to his ramblings about a recipe as he fished out his payment. To herself, she cursed her boyfriend as the echoes of the fight they'd had on her break still bounced off the walls of her memory. Regardless, she pulled her lips tight to present a smile as she handed her old history teacher his change. Living in a small town like Alton Oaks usually meant everyone knew each other and their business.

Mr. Deering, with his aging, slow-moving gait, made his way down the aisle of Prescott Family Grocers and out onto the dark street. As the door closed behind him, the refrigerators kicked on in aisle three and the mechanical hum was taunting. Sara shifted her weight, bit her bottom lip, and sighed, looking at the clock on the wall. Its ticking was deafening as each second filled her with more frustration. She wasn't supposed to close the store herself, and even though there was twice as much to do, it was an incredibly boring job.

The night was warm with the promise of an early summer. The weather was a nice reprieve from the cold nights western Illinois was used to getting. There were so many other things she could be doing instead of working a double shift to cover for her boss who'd decided to take a spur-of-the-moment camping trip. *He has no idea how much he owes me*, she thought with a mischievous grin, her mind flitting back to secrets she kept locked away in her memories.

Looking out the window, she glanced at the usually busy corner of Oak and Main. Now, though, the streets were sleepy and quiet in the small town. She figured that closing the store five minutes early wouldn't matter, and quickly jumped to lock the door and switch the sign to *closed*. Besides, it wasn't the first time she'd closed the store early, but it was the first time she'd done it alone... without someone hungrily waiting for her company.

Flipping off the window lights, the display of waxed produce and sale items drowned in shadows. Sara turned, without a thought, and went through the motions of closing the store: collecting the carts, shelving the put-backs, and cashing out the register. It was a routine she'd completed many times since she'd started working at Prescott's almost two years ago.

The store was eerily quiet. She had turned off the radio that sat by the register hours ago, when she was too mad to make room for music in her cluttered mind. Her face tightened and it grew warm with residual anger as she thought back to the fight she'd had with Calvin. Realizing she'd lost count of the twenty dollar bills in her hands, she let out a frustrated groan and tried to blow the stray piece of hair from her face as she began counting the wad of bills once more. The clock, again, mocked her with each solitary passing second, trimming her patience like a bad haircut.

Usually the store was abuzz with women in the aisles sharing gossip, mothers reigning in their noisy children from the candy display, and the high-pitched squeak of the carts' wheels as customers pushed them up and down the aisles. It suddenly struck Sara at how starkly different the volume was now. She heard her gym shoes squeak slightly on the linoleum floor and the change shift in the till as she carried it to the manager's office where the safe was kept.

Sara stood in front of the heavy, old-fashion safe which was housed behind her boss' desk. The screen saver from the desk top in front of her cast a soft blue hue around the room, and the 1950's style desk lamp illuminated the piles of papers and bound manuals and handbooks. There were two cheap, nondescript picture frames on his desk that reminded him of his wife and his child. They sat on the lawn in front of their small, brick house that wasn't too far away. His wife held their young son in her arms as the breeze rippled the American flag from the mounted flagpole beside them. Sara couldn't help but roll her eyes at the faces in the frames; if only they knew what she knew.

Carefully squatting in front of the safe and dialing in the combination code, Sara felt her tight jeans slip from her narrow hips and she knew her pink leopard-print thong would be visible but didn't care. She never did, whether she was alone or had an audience, despite her boyfriend's plea for decency.

"Of course!" Sara spat as the safe denied the code and refused to open. "Just what I need today," she scoffed, brimming with frustration and hit the side of the solid steel safe. The lack of cooperation from the lock added to her already teeming pot of emotions. She couldn't wait to leave the store, stomp up Oak Street, confront her boyfriend outside his perfect little house, and unleash a raging emotional storm on him.

Moving the till from her arms to the top of the safe, she dramatically entered the code again. Finally, the door gave way and she shoved the till onto the top shelf and made sure the cash-out receipt and deposit bag were visible at the top. Just as she moved to close the safe door, she heard the echo of a noise that wasn't hers. She momentarily froze, her arm leaning on the safe for support as she strained her ears to listen for anything out of place.

A knocking from the mechanisms in the air ducts, the wind whistling from beneath the doors just outside the room, and that infuriating clock ticking away were the only sounds her ears had captured. There was nothing out of the ordinary... unless she counted the beating of her heart that quickly thudded in her ears. Nevertheless, the hairs on her arms stood up beneath the long-sleeved black shirt that she wore under her green Prescott Family Grocers uniform polo. Usually Calvin would be outside, waiting to walk her home, but not today. Probably not ever again after the quarrel they'd had earlier.

Sara bit her lip until she tasted the bitter saltiness of blood in her mouth instead of the nicotine that usually stained her breath. *One, two, three, four...* Sara counted to ten in her head to calm herself down. When she deemed it safe to get up, she slowly straightened her body, still listening to the sounds of the slumbering store.

Cautiously, she walked into the fluorescent-lit hallway and made her way to the double doors of the loading dock to make sure that the back door—where she took her cigarette breaks—was closed and locked. The air there seemed permanently infused with the smell of stale cigarettes and ashes. The scent momentarily calmed her with the thought of a long, calming drag, but the hair on the back of her neck crept across her skin like icicles as shadows seemed to move without a breeze. Rubbing away the goose bumps on the back of her arms, she found herself silently cursing Calvin, but this time it wasn't because of the words he'd chosen to speak to her, it was because he wasn't there waiting for her, to give her a sense of safety.

Hesitantly, she entered the storage room where the fluorescent lights flickered. Shelves of boxed cereal and jars of mayonnaise and pickles cast odd shadows that danced in the aisle in front of her. "Of course, the lights are flickering," Sara muttered under her breath. "All I need now is the theme music to *Psycho* playing in the background."

As she pretended not to tip-toe through the eerie scene, Sara tried to keep her cool, but inside, her heart beat faster and her mouth grew dry. She couldn't shake off the uneasy feeling that gripped her soul, and she tried to convince herself that it was only due to the emotional day she was having. Sara didn't want to admit that it was her primal instincts trying to warn her that she wasn't alone, so she buried it deep beneath her boiling kettle of poisoned opinions.

Her rubber-soled footsteps sounded louder than they were as she walked to the metal door that led to the dumpsters in the alley. Normally, Sara wouldn't have checked this door, but she'd had a rough day and had taken too many cigarette breaks, and that noise...

Pushing against the cool metal doors that were covered in grime and dents, a small tremor of shock shook through Sara when she found the door unlocked. Her heart skipped a beat and it thudded loudly in her ears as she pulled the doors shut and locked them with an echoing click, double checking its security before turning on her heels. *The sooner I can get out of here, the better,* she thought to herself, trying to shake off the fierce chills that wanted to violently rip down her spine in warning. Walking briskly and waving away the dread that was coming at her in waves, she made her way to the locker room to grab her purse so she could hightail it home.

Flipping on the light switch, she jumped in surprise at the figure that stood before her. Her breath caught in her throat and her heart skipped a beat before it thudded deafeningly in her ears. Sara found herself face-to-face with a familiar figure in an unfamiliar setting. Before she could ask why or how, she was attacked by the person she thought she knew and could trust.

There wasn't much of a fight. Sara's head smashed onto the corner of the employee's break table and she crashed to the floor with a *crack* as the attacker lunged forward. Luckily, for Sara's sake, she was knocked unconscious so that she didn't suffer too much as the assailant pierced her body thirty-seven times.

As the attacker finished the job, they wrapped the knife carefully in a piece of cloth. Then they washed their hands in the employee's sink, where someone's coffee mug had been soaking with the pink flower-scented soap every employee used before returning to work.

Turning to leave the scene, the attacker looked back with a smug nod at their work, noting that the blood from Sara's head injury trailed down to meet the blood pooling from the stab wounds on the black and white linoleum floor. They deemed the job well done and long overdue.

CHAPTER 1

He hadn't followed me down the stairs and out into the heat of the day, for which I was thankful, dare I say relieved. He had banged on our apartment door for almost an hour before giving up—at least I was worth almost an hour. It was all the time I needed to get my affairs in order and make this life-changing decision. Had it only been a little over an hour ago when my life was normal?

Standing outside the apartment building, with traffic whizzing down the street and the sun already starting to activate my sweat glands, I pulled out my cell phone and called the person who could fix almost anything.

After three rings, she answered in her peppy voice that always greeted my phone calls—even the three A.M. drunk dials back in college. My lips moved to tell her, but my voice had disappeared. Dread coated my stomach as I realized what I was about to do. "Are you there? Is this a butt-dial?" she asked with a lightness to her voice.

Her warm tone gave me the courage to speak and I blurted it out, "I'm finally doing it, Sadie," I said breathlessly into the phone to my best friend. "I'm moving back to Alton Oaks."

In the silence that followed. I could just picture her gripping the phone, processing my words as she slowly opened the car door or grabbed her mid-shift coffee break from the hospital cafeteria. Unlike me, she'd decided to stay in our tiny hometown after college. She suggested I move back on several different occasions over the years, but I always openly laughed in her face.

The gap in our conversation seemed longer than it actually was and I bit my lip waiting for her response. Finally, she replied, "Well, it's about damn time, Charlotte May Parker. We miss you."

Relief rushed out of me in the form of a sigh. Once again, I looked up at the apartment and to the entrance door. There was still no sign of him.

Sadie then added, as an afterthought, "Does that mean Jackson is coming too?" I knew she didn't like him, but it didn't stop me from marrying him—boy, did I learn my lesson.

"No," I let the word trail out of my mouth hesitantly. I knew once the word ended there would be questions, and I wasn't ready for questions. A breeze rushed down the street and lightly tossed a few locks of my long brown hair into my face. Pushing it back into place, I held a hand to my forehead to block the sun as I searched the street for my cab, bracing myself for Sadie's response.

"No?" She sounded intrigued and hungry for gossip—a trait one must have to live in Alton Oaks.

"I'll tell you when I see you," I said, pushing my bangs from my eyes. They were growing too fast. I'd had an appointment to get them cut after work tomorrow... but not anymore.

"When will that be?" Sadie sounded as if she was getting the raw end of the deal. Ever since I graduated college, I came home to visit maybe once a year and it was never enough time, according to Sadie.

"That depends." I let the two words drag out of my mouth with hesitation.

"On what?" she asked. I knew her so well, I would have made a bet that she was lifting a skeptical eyebrow on the other side of the phone call.

With each question Sadie asked, I was getting closer

to the truth and I wasn't sure I was ready to admit it yet. Once again I threw a furtive glance towards the entrance of the apartment building, hoping I wouldn't see Jackson. I tapped my suitcase with my toe and adjusted my old backpacking backpack that weighed down my shoulders, as I anxiously waited for my cab. "It depends on if you want to pick me up from the airport in Chicago tonight or if I have to take the shuttle bus."

Alton Oaks was at least a two hour drive from Chicago so everyone flew into Davenport, Iowa. However, the soonest, cheapest flight I could find left in an hour and flew into the Windy City. The wealthier residents of Alton Oaks would charter a plane to Sheridan—a town about the size of ours—which had a private air strip and was only five miles away. I was asking a lot from Sadie, but I didn't want to be alone on the four hour bus shuttle.

"Charli!" she exclaimed. Her voice was shrill with surprise and I could imagine her eyebrows raising, her mouth opening, and her arm reaching out to hit me, only I wasn't there. Despite her reaction, it was good to hear my old nickname again, like a hug welcoming me home. During my years outside Alton Oaks, I went by Charlotte, but it was always someone I wasn't. "Tonight? Are you sure? Does your mother know?"

I sighed. I missed Sadie and really needed my best friend. "I promise, when I see you I'll tell you everything."

"Okay," she agreed. "I'll be there. Text me the details of your flight."

A smile crossed my lips with the thought of Sadie being there for me on the other side of this trip. It reassured me; I wasn't sure if leaving Albuquerque so abruptly was the right thing to do, but I couldn't stay. I had to get away.

As I watched the cab pull up at the curb in front of me, I pocketed the cell phone. The driver stowed my backpack and suitcase into the trunk; though it wasn't all of my earthly possessions, it was all I could gather, all that was important, essential. Turning on my heels, I lifted my head to take one last look at the apartment that had been my home for the past four years. The home I had built with Jackson. The dream I thought I had always wanted.

I let the New Mexico sun warm my skin one last time and then climbed into the back of the cab. Watching the familiar sights of my everyday life disappear—the billboard advertising a Mexican restaurant, the mural on the side of the brick store, the artist with his easel on the corner—I let the tears fall. I bid farewell to the life I thought I knew.

CHAPTER 2

Unless you're a bicycling enthusiast or have an affinity for canals, you've probably never heard of Alton Oaks. My hometown has a historic downtown on the Whett River Canal Trail. I don't mean to brag, but it's rated second only to Chicago's Lake Shore Drive for its scenic trail. Cars and motor homes carrying bicycle racks litter the streets when they're not covered in snow or ice.

I grew up in the Alton house at the dead end of Oak Street. Canaries—our term for out of town canal seekers—always drove up Oak Street from Terryville and missed the turn onto US Highway 16 and ended up in our driveway. My childhood was spattered with lost visitors ringing our doorbell during dinner, or we'd see them climb down the wooden stairs, scratching their heads and holding maps as Sadie and I walked up the driveway from school.

Behind the house was a forest of oak trees—all that's left as most oaks were cut down for farmland and now reside in the architecture of the buildings in our historic downtown. There was still a trail that leads though the trees that connects the Alton house with Gnarled Circle Road, the swanky housing development where Sadie grew up. It's considered the "rich" part of town where everyone follows strict picture-perfect, cookie-cutter guidelines set forth by their Homeowners Association. Sadie moved to downtown Alton Oaks after college, which is much newer and much closer to the brand new hospital—St. Collete's—where she works as a nurse in the pediatric ward.

It was that trail between our houses, nestled between the old oak trees, where Sadie and I spent a good deal of our adolescence. We buried a time capsule beneath one of the trees, built a fort out of fallen branches and twigs after the storm of '95, and it was where we would seek shelter from the sweltering sun on those hot summer days, sucking on melting popsicles.

And here we were again. Walking that same trail many years later, just as the sun was rising. Sadie and I drove through the night from Chicago and took a long walk through the streets we grew up in, talking about what had happened to my marriage.

We had walked down Oak Street, through the dark and deserted historic downtown on Main Street where I cried through Town Circle. I let out anger as the sun began breaking the horizon and reflected on the river. I stomped through the playground at our old elementary school, briefly crying again, then slumping on the swings in emotional exhaustion.

Sadie had given me a pep talk as we walked up Gnarled Circle Drive, squeezing my shoulder, nudging my elbow, and having me relive memories of a happier time.

Now that the sun was breaking through the oak trees, I wasn't as bitter or teary, though I'm sure I looked as horrible as I felt.

"You can't think of this as a step backwards," Sadie said as the morning light began playing in her auburn hair. She was a few inches shorter than me, the top of her head barely measuring up to my shoulder. But what she lacked in height, she made up for in spunk. She had joined the high school volleyball team to keep me company at try-outs, and ended up being one of the fiercest players—even earning a partial volleyball scholarship at Loyola.

"Moving back home isn't something shameful. I think it's smart," Sadie said, sitting on the trunk of a young fallen tree. "You need a support system right now and to not be in that toxic environment, until you figure everything out. You need to focus on you and what you want—what's going to help you sort through this."

I was still wearing flip flops and a pair of shorts that had served me well in New Mexico, but were chilly for this April Illinois morning. Goosebumps erupted down my legs as I looked at Sadie, unsure of her words. "But I quit my job. I left nearly all my belongings behind and I left my husband. I just... left. That's not how a twenty-eight year old woman should act."

Sadie stood up and did her best to look me straight in the eye. "Leaving isn't always the wrong thing to do. Sometimes staying is much worse." We walked into a patch of sunlight and I lingered, letting the warmth wash away my goose bumps.

"It's not like he hit me or anything. Maybe I over-reacted?" I said, my hands balled into fists, pushing deep into the pockets of the sweater.

When Sadie and I would dive head first into her swimming pool, her mom used to give us 'The Look.' One raised eyebrow and lips pursed to the side of her face. Her expression said, "Are you kidding me? You know better than that." I don't know if it's genetics or years of practice, but Sadie copied the look perfectly.

"Look," she said, shifting her weight to one leg. "I'm not saying you're never going back to him or that you're divorcing him, but you need a break. He would ignore you, go missing for hours—sometimes days at a time, and then he cheated on you with your neighbor. No one, especially you, deserves that. He was feet away from you—just the other side of your bedroom wall—that's just..." Sadie groaned in frustration and balled her fists, mumbling her own set of G-rated profanities.

Deep in my heart I knew she was right, but I couldn't keep thinking about what I could have done differently to keep our marriage healthy and happy. I was explaining this as we emerged from the trees and walked up to my mother's house. We sat on the wooden paint-chipped stairs like we often did as teenagers, usually with ice cream tacos or a caffeinated beverage.

"Marriage isn't a puppy that you take to obedience school, potty train, and keep a bowl of food and water for it. It's a two-way street, a team effort. You could have done a million things differently, but if he didn't want to work for it, or put in the time and dedication, you would be in the same place," Sadie said with conviction. She had had much more experience with romantic relationships than I had so I had to think she knew what she was talking about.

The sun was rising behind the house and we were bathed in the cold shadows left from the night. I pulled the NIU sweater I'd stolen from Sadie's backseat over my legs as I hugged them, letting fresh tears blur my vision. "Why wasn't I good enough?" I asked, feeling a hot bead of despair race down my tear-stained cheek and onto my neck as I stared at my cold toes.

Sadie sat closer to me and put an arm around my shoulder. The rough material of her jeans brushed against my bare leg and her Riley C. Shepard High School volleyball coach windbreaker momentarily kept away the biting chill that ate through my sweater. "Don't do that to yourself," she said, resting her head on my shoulder and rubbing my arm. "You *are* good enough. He's just an idiot who doesn't see that."

I let myself cry for a few moments, feeling safe as I hugged my best friend on the stairs of my childhood home. "He might never see it," Sadie continued. "But that doesn't mean you aren't good enough. Mark my words, Charli May, one day someone will go out of their way to show you just how good you are and that you are worth it."

The words Sadie said rolled off my shoulders, but I just couldn't take them to heart yet, so I tucked them away, hoping one day I'd be brave enough to visit them again.

"You'll be okay," Sadie said as we parted. The warmth she temporarily gave me vanished as a new set of goose bumps rolled in. "It'll take some time."

I nodded, wiping my eyes and nose with the sleeves of her sweater which was already damp with tears. "Mom will be up any minute," I said, peering behind me at the gauzy drapes in the windows.

"You better get in there before she makes you go on a five mile walk with her." Sadie smiled and nudged me with her knee before getting up from the stairs. "Get lots of sleep. I'll come by this afternoon."

Nodding, I stood up and hugged her. "Thank you," I said, breathing in the fruity scent of her hair.

"Anytime," she said, pulling apart from the hug. She began walking down the driveway towards Oak Street when she turned and said with a bright smile, "Besides, this way I get to see you every day."

CHAPTER 3

My mother was bouncing down the stairs in her bright green gym shoes, black jogging pants and a highly reflective, bright yellow, long-sleeve shirt, as I walked into the house. "Good morning, Charli," she said and greeted me with huge sloppy kisses on both cheeks as she reached the bottom of the stairs. She wore a Chicago Cubs baseball cap that covered most of her short blonde hair.

With her hands on my shoulders, she looked me in the eye, and I expected a million questions. After all, I'd only left her a rushed, slightly hectic, voicemail about coming back to Alton Oaks. When she couldn't reach me for more information, she'd called Sadie who'd filled her in on the situation. My heart raced and I pushed back tears as I braced for impact, but she only said, "Have something to eat with me and you can go on upstairs and get some sleep. You must be exhausted." As she walked into the kitchen, I realized I was holding my breath and let it out, surprised by her reaction.

We sat across from each other at the kitchen table, the song of the birds outside and the crunching of our food were the only sounds. Over a slice of toast covered in blueberry yogurt, I watched my mom eat an apple with almond butter, her attention on an article in *The Oak Leaf Press*, our local newspaper. Once in a while, she'd look at me and smile when grabbing another apple slice or turning the page; it gave me an uneasy feeling. I felt like a dying animal and she was looking for the right time to go in for the kill.

She didn't say anything, or ask me any questions, which frightened me a little. My mother was known as the Queen of Gossip in Alton Oaks. I expected her to grill me with questions, but they never came. The burning acid of anxiety hit my stomach and I pushed away the plate that held what was left of my toast. My mother looked up and raised an eyebrow in question.

"Not hungry," I said, pushing my chair out from the table, the wooden legs scraping across the laminate floor. My face was encrusted in dried tears, my eyes burned with exhaustion, and I was still cold. I just wanted to give up for a few hours under a blanket and sleep. "I'm tired," I mumbled, while avoiding eye contact.

Mom nodded, reaching for my plate and turned towards the sink. Leaving the kitchen without giving away any information was too easy. When I reached the bottom of the stairs, I heard her voice cut through the hallway between us. "We'll talk later, Charli, okay?"

"Uh huh," I said, grabbing the banister and mentally preparing myself to be cornered by her in the near future.

Stopping in the bathroom to wash my face, I looked in the mirror. I felt no emotion looking at the girl with the mess of brown hair, including overgrown bangs and red-rimmed green eyes. I was numb. No longer was I angry or jealous or lost or unhappy. I was a shell.

Walking into my old bedroom, I pulled back the covers on my bed. Slipping off my sandals in two swift motions, I tucked myself deeply into the bedding and ignored the rising sun. It didn't take long before I fell into a world where I forgot myself.

It was late in the afternoon, when the sun cast long shadows into my bedroom window, when I finally sat up and pulled that old childhood quilt off of me. My head felt empty—the thoughts and tortured memories that had plagued me were temporarily gone as I fought through the fog of unconsciousness.

Listening to the birds in the tree outside my window, I ran my fingers through the knots in my hair. Pulling my hair into a ponytail, I surveyed my bedroom, which hadn't changed much since I'd left for college; the air still smelled like cheap candy-scented body lotion.

An old, massive computer monitor sat on my dust-covered desk, with a set of 1960-era encyclopedias on the shelf above it. A boy band poster still hung on the back of my door with a blue moon and stars-themed bathrobe on the hook. And that ancient bulky CD player I'd bought after saving money for a year in middle school, sat on my dresser with a homemade music mix still sitting in the tape deck.

Before I could start reminiscing on where my life had gone wrong, I threw on a pair of sweatpants I'd found in my closet that bore the name of my high school, and climbed down the loudly creaking stairs in search of food. Everything in the house creaked or moaned or fell apart.

My great-great-grandfather, Andrew Alton, had built this house when he established Alton Oaks in 1914. It was a historic house, but it was falling apart and my mother and father never seemed to want to fix it up entirely. In the nineties, my dad and Uncle Randy—who is now the town mayor—fixed up two of the bedrooms where he and my twin cousins stayed after my aunt died. Then, a few Christmases ago, Mom talked about renovating the living room, but nothing ever happened.

Due to the state of the house, my family spent the summers on the front porch and the winters in the kitchen or the screened-in back porch. It was covered in layers of blurry weatherized plastic and musty wool blankets huddled around the potbelly stove. The smell of burning wood and wet blankets was infused in the threadbare couch and deteriorating wicker furniture that decorated the space.

As I descended the stairs, I noticed the plastic draping hanging from the door frame that led into the living room gently swaying in the evening breeze. I shivered at how cool the air was compared to what I was used to in New Mexico. I heard the faucet running in the kitchen and the soft sound of the radio playing on the counter.

"Hi, Mom," I said, taking a seat at the small wooden table in the corner of the kitchen.

"Hey, Charli," Mom said through a smile. "I saved you some dinner." She nodded to the left and said, "There's a plate in the oven."

Determining whether or not the plate of food was a ploy to get information, I watched her put the last dish in the drying rack and wipe her hands on the dish towel hanging beside the oven. "Uncle Randy and Jenna are both dying to see you." She laid her arms on the back of the chair across from me and clasped her hands. "They came over for dinner. You should pop on over." She glanced at her watch and added, "It's not too late."

I nodded. My stomach growled loudly so I pulled the plate from the oven and sat at the table. "Maybe," I replied.

The same old blue and white country-themed plastic place mats from my childhood sat at the table and I picked up the rooster and hen salt and pepper shakers that sat between them. Mom had found them at a garage sale during a family trip to Galena when my sister, Bailey, was still in diapers. My brother Alex and I always used to pretend they were action figures: Helga the Hen who fights salty crimes and Regulus the

Rooster who peppers the plans of any crime-doer through the amazing power of sneezing. I grinned at the memories I had with my brother.

My mother was a newborn health nut and the plate of meatloaf, string beans, and mashed potatoes surprised me. "Went a little wild on dinner, did you?" I asked.

"No." She gently shook her head with an amused smile. "That's a seitan loaf with a chickpea gravy. I mashed some cauliflower, and added seasoned coconut oil to the steamed string beans. It's good; try it," she encouraged.

Trying not to make a face, I salted the "meatloaf" and added a dash of pepper to the "mashed potatoes." (Helga and Regulus once again find themselves fighting a crime, but this time it was against imposter food!) Mom pulled out the chair and sat down across from me, asking, "When was the last time you saw your cousin, Jenna? Must have been last Christmas, right?"

This past December was the first Christmas I didn't come home to visit since my Peace Corps term had ended. Jackson had wanted to drive up to Colorado for the holiday and the idea seemed so romantic to me. I forfeited a holiday trip to Illinois only to be left alone at the ski lodge when Jackson "got lost" on a snowshoeing hike for two of the four nights we spent there. It had been over a year since I'd seen any member of my family.

"Yeah, something like that," I replied, guilt stabbing my chest with the reminder that I chose to skip Christmas last year. Avoiding eye contact, I stuck my spoon in and out of the gravy and mashed cauliflower until they made a sucking sound.

My mother leaned in. "You doin' okay? Do you want to talk about it?" Her voice was sincere but it felt staged; she was trying hard not to be so pushy and nosy.

My dear mother wanted to be supportive without prying, which was quite a feat for her, since I'm sure her "Gossip Club" were prodding her with questions. If she hadn't already showed up at my sister's house down the street (only acres away from ours), with a basketful of questions, or plagued Sadie's phone with messages while I was sleeping, I'd be surprised.

I nodded with a smile. "I'm not hungry. I think I'll take a walk down Oak," I said, standing up.

Without skipping a beat, she asked, "In that case, do you want to stop at the grocers and pick up some frozen strawberries for your mother?" She lifted an eyebrow in question.

My mother had been on a health kick for the past year and a half when she'd had a mini-heart attack in the middle of Thanksgiving dinner. I hadn't been there, but my older brother is a doctor and helped her plan a healthier lifestyle. After thirty-plus years of smoking, drinking three cans of soda a day, and eating fried and fatty meals, she quit it all and now eats vegan and exercises like an Olympian. I guessed the fruits were for her post-workout protein smoothie in the morning.

I nodded and grabbed a sweater before leaving through the squeaking hinges of the screen door that smacked the wooden frame when it closed. We lived on the east side of town, about half a mile past the street for Gnarled Circle Drive when traveling on Oak Street. Besides the Alton House and a lot of open land, there were only six other houses before you hit the schools and crossed into the more populated area of town.

My little sister, Bailey Rae, had moved into the house closest to my mother's. She'd married Carter, a firefighter, a year before my own marriage. They have a four year old son, Eli. My cousin Jenna, her husband Mark, and my uncle Randy live across from her. Further down the road, an empty house sat between

Jenna's and her twin sister Jillian's. Mr. and Mrs. Kratsky were an old couple who occupied the house the furthest away and they always gave out full size candy bars at Halloween. Mr. Kratsky also fixed bicycles in his garage for the locals, which was much cheaper than the tourist-driven bike shops downtown.

Next to Bailey was the Vega's house. I went to school with their son Jake, but I wasn't sure if they still owned it. There used to be a ceramic horse pulling a cart full of flowers that sat on their lawn for years, but was missing now. The house looked like it had been painted recently—a deep powder blue (or was it always that color?) and the roof had dark shingles which I doubt had seen many winters.

As I studied the Vega's house on my walk, my cell phone pinged that I had a message.

Sadie: Almost out of work. Ice cream and a movie?
Me: Sure! Meet me at Prescott's?
Sadie: On my way in 15.

The walk to the grocers couldn't have taken more than thirty minutes. I stood on the corner of Oak & Main, just outside Prescott's Family Grocer's and waited for Sadie. I liked the fact that the town was small enough where a lot of people walked to the places they had to go. Not many people needed a car, unless they were working outside of town, which is why we didn't have a traffic light, just a four way stop on Oak & Main, which was mainly for the Canaries. I took a deep breath of the river whose scent bathed the town. How did I not get homesick for this place?

As I waited for Sadie, I people-watched. Many of them were headed north, to the park or to the only restaurant in town, Oakies. My dad was the manager of Oakies Bar & Grill which was at the end of the block, just across from Froz T's ice cream, and I contemplated stopping in to say hi, but thought against it as it was the dinner rush and he would be busy.

It was dark now and the street lamps were burning bright. I stood at the far side of the building where some employees took their breaks and where the dumpsters sat. Sadie had a huge crush on Nick Simons in high school and he worked at the grocer's part time. Sadie and I would nonchalantly walk by every chance we got, just in case he wanted to profess his secret love to her.

Now there was a young girl with blonde hair and brown roots, wearing the Prescott uniform, and talking to a boy in a Chicago Cubs jersey and a pair of jeans. The safety lights on the side of the building showed them clearly. His posture hunched and his hands dug deep into his pockets. The blonde listened as she smoked a cigarette. Soon, though, she began to yell and wave her hands at the boy, but he held the same helpless stance. I couldn't quite hear what was being said, but the girl finally stomped back into the store, slamming the door behind her.

The boy stood staring at the door for a few moments and I tried to look interested in a crack on the sidewalk so he wouldn't know I'd watched the entire scene. But I was an Alton; I was nosy. I picked up my head as he turned away from the building. Our eyes met for a moment and I felt myself blush. He looked helpless, but a fierce upset rose in his eyes. I turned my head down Oak Street where I saw Sadie approaching.

She came from the west and the sky still had some color where it brushed along the horizon. She still wore her scrubs and it looked like it had been a long day; her normally straight auburn hair was in disarray, as if she had run her hands through it several times. "Rough shift?" I asked as she caught up to me.

Sadie rolled her eyes. "I wasn't supposed to work

today, but there was an accident with a city bus in Terryville so they needed extra hands. You ready for an ice cream taco?" Sadie asked, nudging me toward Froz T's. I couldn't wait to hold the waffle cone shell filled with soft-serve ice cream and let the hot fudge collect the bits of nuts and green tinted coconut shavings as it oozed out the back and down my hand.

"Yeah, but I have to stop in at Prescott's first to get some fruit," I shared regretfully.

Sadie looked longingly down the street towards the growing line outside of Froz T's walk-up window. Their outside lights flooded the sidewalk and the soft sound of pop music drifted down the street from their speakers.

"Your mom?" she asked.

"We could take a page out of her book," I said, nudging Sadie with my elbow. "We could have a fruit salad instead—"

"Instead of an ice cream taco? Are you insane?" An incredulous look sat upon Sadie's face and she grabbed my elbow, walking towards the store. "You are lucky you have me to keep you on the straight and narrow." She reached the door and ushered me inside. "Now buy that fruit so we can go to Froz T's and stuff our faces right and proper. Honestly, how have you lived so long without me being a part of your everyday decisions?"

I laughed and Sadie led me quickly through the store; we were at the cash register within seconds. The blonde I'd seen smoking a cigarette minutes earlier was at the register with a scratched up plastic name plate bearing the name *Sara* pinned to her polo shirt.

Sara entered the cost of the fruit into the old, bulky register as Sadie picked up a celebrity news magazine that was on display and leafed through the pages. "I can't believe they actually got married," she remarked as Sara tinkered with the register and bagged the fruit.

"Who?" I asked, peering over her shoulder. I was never one to pick up celebrity tabloids in my adult life, but Sadie and I used to check the newsstand at least once a week as teenagers. We were really into the behind-the-band music articles.

"Galvin Kismet and his girlfriend from forever ago," she reported, showing me the cover. A much older version of the man in one of our favorite bands graced the cover with his girlfriend who only got more beautiful with age.

"Remember that song?" I asked, instantly being transported to middle school when Galvin's band had that song that took over the summer of 2000. Sadie and I spent all summer listening to it in her backyard, obsessing over the German rock band.

"Oh god!" Sadie exclaimed. She started mumbling incoherent words to the familiar tune until she hit the chorus and we both belted out the lyrics dramatically, "I was cuttin' the rain, putting off the pain. Soakin' in regrets, hardly payin' respects, living in distain. Yeah, I was cuttin' the rain."

"Hey!" Sara's voice punctured our nostalgic bubble as Sadie and I let giggles slip through our lips. Sara's eyes were dangerously close to eye rolling and her lips were thin with impatience. "You want that too or just the fruit?" she asked, jerking her thumb at the magazine with a tone so sharp it could have pierced through glass.

Feeling like we were being chastised by a mother, Sadie gently slipped the magazine back onto the rack and shook her head. Sara was at least ten years younger than us, but her agitation was like a volcano about to erupt. I let it go because I figured it had something to do with the scene I'd witnessed earlier.

Without making eye contact, I handed Sara a payment and then grabbed the bag of fruit. With our heads down, trying not to laugh, Sadie and I made it back out the door and onto the pavement where we continued singing the chorus of "Cuttin' the Rain," feeling like teenagers again, as we made our way down to Froz T's.

It had been a long time since I'd felt that free. I looked over at Sadie who had started dancing to the lyrics and I was thankful for having her support and friendship through the good and these unanticipated difficult times in my life.

CHAPTER 4

After a proper meal of ice cream tacos, Sadie and I sat on the curb, letting the cement slowly steal our warmth, as we ate a plate of s'more nachos. "I miss this," I admitted, pulling a graham cracker from the marshmallow sauce and added a few extra chocolate chips before stuffing it in my mouth.

"Me too," Sadie agree and wiped a gob of marshmallow from her chin.

We shared a brownie-batter milk shake that sat in a large white Styrofoam container between us. I took a large gulp and then laughed.

"What?" Sadie asked, breaking off another portion of graham cracker. A group of high school kids had gathered with their own Froz T treats at a picnic table a few yards from us. They had started laughing and it brought me back to a simpler time.

Smiling passively, I shared, "You're a nurse, Sadie."

"Yes," she agreed, confused. "Well done. You've been paying attention," she added jokingly.

I rolled my eyes. "You have to be the unhealthiest healthcare worker ever. Didn't you learn about nutrition and stuff?" Sadie always had a knack for sugar-coated plans.

Sadie was dipping her finger in the marshmallow sauce, scraping it from the edges so that none of it was wasted. She popped it in her mouth dramatically. "Charli, darling," she started, wiping her hands on a sticky napkin, "when it comes to you and me and our particular brand of crazy, sugar is the only prescription."

I laughed. "That sounds like an excuse," I admitted, stealing the last of the chocolate chips and popping them in my mouth.

Sadie tilted her head questioningly and asked, "You can slurp celery sticks if you want," she paused to sigh at the empty container that only held the crumbs and sticky residue that once was s'more nachos, "but sometimes ice cream tacos and gummy bears are the only sugar-coated treats you get in life."

Her eyes turned dark for a moment and I didn't want a serious conversation. She was, however, my best friend and perhaps it was my turn to be there for her. Before I could dive into the topic, she looked up and asked, "Do you want to hang out for a while?"

Holding my full belly, I didn't relish the idea of walking all the way home just yet. And, I think, she needed me. Or I needed her. Either way, we weren't ready to part. "Yeah. Got anything for a stomach ache?" I asked as we stood up. I brushed the dirt off my sweatpants, and hoped feeling would return to my backside as soon as we started walking.

Her face was now bright with animation. "Awe," Sadie said, turning to face me in the lamp light. "We need to get you and your stomach back into training." She patted my belly as if I was pregnant. "Come on," she added, leading me towards her apartment. "We can soak in a few *American Horror Story* episodes while taking shots of Pepto."

As we walked toward the intersection of Oak and Main, we talked about our favorite TV show. (When we discovered we could stream the show anytime, we had allowed ourselves three episodes a week. Sometimes we'd watch an episode together while on the phone or via video chat to keep each other honest in our viewing habits.) Our voices dropped as we saw two figures in the streetlight by Prescott's Family Grocer.

Our friendly check-out lady, Sara, was still at work and she stood basked in the yellow glow of a weak security light, enveloped in a halo of cigarette smoke. She wasn't alone either. The boy in the Cubs jersey was gone. He was replaced by a beefy stranger in a black leather jacket who leaned up against a motorcycle as he took a long drag of a cigarette a few feet from her in the parking lot.

"Oh la la," Sadie sang just loud enough for me to hear as she linked her arm in mine. "Who's the hottie with the body?" she asked, nodding and nudged my attention towards the motorcycle.

I shrugged my shoulders, feigning an air of indifference, but studied him out of the corner of my eye as we walked past. His whole aura screamed wild, danger, and excitement. His dark hair was slicked back, but pieces fell in front of his amber eyes in the streetlight. His leather jacket squeaked slightly when he moved his arm to take a drag on his cigarette. Our eyes met briefly as he pulled the cigarette from his lips when we walked by, a mere ten feet from them. Chills tickled my backbone, though I wasn't sure if it was from a foreboding tension, or from a foreign excitement.

Sadie rented the second floor of a house behind the grocers. It was set up like an apartment and Mrs. Flanagan lived downstairs, but Sadie had her own set of external stairs via the back entrance. Her landlady played her TV too loud and hit the ceiling with a broom whenever Sadie walked around too much. Ever since her parents had retired to Florida, though, Sadie decorated it with sunflowers and French paraphernalia and called it home.

After we left the light from the parking lot, I still felt a pair of eyes watching me. I tried to shrug them off as Sara's angry daggers for Sadie and me momentarily interrupting her cigarette break, but I knew that wasn't it. As we started ascending the long set of wooden stairs to the kitchen entrance of Sadie's apartment, I turned to glance at the pair still sitting in the parking lot. Sara talked while waving her cigarette-clenched hand, her head turned from me and back to the man in black. The stranger, however, coolly leaning on his motorcycle, had watched us climb the stairs and I could still feel his eyes watching me, but tried to shrug them off as we walked into the warm, vanilla-scented air of Sadie's tiny kitchen.

After several heart-pounding episodes of *American Horror Story*, I decided not to walk home. While the credits and creepy music scrolled across the screen, I yawned. "Is it cool if I just crash here?" I asked Sadie from my spot on the over-sized wing chair that was lumpy in all the right places. "It's dark," I protested, sinking deeper into the safety of the chair. "And it's the middle of the night."

Sadie shrugged. Her knees were to her chest and the sleeves on the oversized gray sweater were rolled up so they didn't cover her hands. "I'll let you borrow a flashlight. No biggie," she said and yawned from her seat on the couch. She reached for the remote and turned the television off so that the shadows grew louder around us.

Looking around the apartment, I noted that besides the glow from the clock on the microwave and cable box under the television, the only other light was from Prescott's parking lot which sifted through the kitchen curtains behind us, sending my imagination into a fit of unrealistic possibilities. "And down unlit dirt roads," I added.

Sadie was only protesting in good humor. The wind outside blew dancing shadows across her face as she talked, and I nearly jumped when the motor of the refrigerator kicked on, sending an otherwise gentle hum across the room. "I'll make sure it's a powerful flashlight. Full batteries," she added, stretching her arms in front of her and planting her feet on the floor.

"Past the town cemetery!" I added in mock disbelief. Shivering at the thought, I tried not to let my mind wander to the dark, mysterious, and scary ideas the show had buried into my head. I picked my feet up off the floor and tucked my knees into my chest.

"I think I have a crucifix somewhere," she replied, looking around her apartment. For a moment I thought she was being serious—like she had other plans or was expecting company. My mouth parted at the thoughts racing around my mind, especially if I had to walk home. Then, chucking a throw pillow at my head, she laughed. "Oh, of course you can stay, Charli!" and she laughed, rising from the couch.

After Sadie closed her bedroom door, still laughing at her little joke, the night grew darker and the darkness seemed to hover like predators as I settled onto the couch. I pulled the afghan she kept draped over the furniture on top of my head, wincing at the unfamiliar sounds in the night. Turning the television back on to chase away the vindictive shadows and menacing sounds, I fell asleep hugging a pillow in the comforting glow of infomercials.

When the sun struggled to pour through the window shades, Sadie emerged from her room in her work scrubs and in a sunny disposition. "Good morning," she said in her charming Cinderella voice as she walked past me towards the open kitchen.

Peeling the blanket from my head, I responded in a flat voice, "You no speak." I raised a hand as if it would stop her. "Coffee first. Words later." The past forty-eight hours had a been a whirlwind of emotions and with the haunting images of ghosts and blood from our binge-watching session fresh in my head, I hadn't gotten a lot of sleep.

Sadie let out a chuckle as she reached into her kitchen cabinets for a granola bar. "I have some time if you want to buy me a morning coffee," hinted Sadie, tossing a granola bar into my lap. "But you should get this to your mom before they defrost," she said pulling the fruit we'd bought last night from the freezer.

After grunting in agreement, I slipped on my shoes and stumbled out the back door with Sadie. As she locked the door behind her, I put my hair into a pony tail and looked out over Alton Oaks. The cool morning breeze was crisp and hit my face like a splash of cold water as I looked out over a bird's eye view of Main Street. The Buzz coffee shop shared a building with the bookstore on Main, a five minute walk from Sadie's. I looked down the street, across the rooftops to survey the number of people populating The Buzz this morning, but stopped when the crowd outside Prescott's caught my eye.

"What's going on at Prescott's?" I asked, picking at the peeling paint from the support beam on her wooden porch.

Sadie dropped her keys in her purse and let the screen door shut behind her. "Probably the Pineapple Bowl," she said shrugging, joining me as I leaned out over the ledge which squeaked slightly under my weight. "Jim usually holds it around this time, but I haven't seen any signs for it," she shared, turning towards the stairs.

"What's a Pineapple Bowl?" I asked through a yawn, descending the stairs slowly, next to Sadie.

"You remember Jim Browski? He went to school with your brother; I think he was a year older than him?" She glanced in my direction but I only shivered at the crisp air invading my sweater. "He bought Prescott's five or six years ago from his uncle. Every spring he holds a Pineapple Bowl. He has the local sellers he distributes—like Aunt Mary's Jam, North Wind Candles, and Puppy Paws Bakery—each hide a pineapple sticker inside one of their products. Whoever finds the sticker gets a prize. It boosts sales for him and helps the local economy, so everyone's really into it. That's the only time there's ever a line outside Prescott's, unless it's time to pick up the Thanksgiving turkey and it's not November."

We had left the stairs and ended on the blacktop behind Prescott's. Just as we were about to shrug off the crowd to the Pineapple Bowl, a patrol car and ambulance discreetly pulled up at the curb. I nudged Sadie with my shoulder and jerked my chin to the far right. "Is that normal for the Pineapple Bowl?" I asked.

Sadie's eyebrows furrowed together as she bit her bottom lip. "Fancy some of Aunt Mary's Jam?" she asked, grabbing my elbow and making a ninety-degree turn to check out the crowd. Though she'd spent a few years outside of Alton Oaks to get her nursing degree, she was still drawn to small-town drama like my uncle Randy was drawn to the scent of barbecue ribs on any grill in town.

When we reached the group of people bundled up in their layers and sweaters, morning cyclists also stopped to gather gossip as they zipped up their Northface jackets. "What time is it?" I asked Sadie, recognizing barely a few faces in the crowd.

"Almost half past eight," Sadie reported, illuminating the screen of her cell phone. "Prescott's should be open by now."

"Haven't you heard?" a brown-haired women with gray streaks asked as she turned to face Sadie and me.

She had a worn-out face with bags under her eyes and wore a very large Chicago Bears sweater that nearly came to her knees. She looked familiar, but I couldn't quite place where in my past she was from.

Sadie shook her head and moved closer to the woman for more information. "Alexis Quinn went to open the store this morning for a six a.m. shipment and found Sara Zimmer dead on the floor of the employee locker room. Blood all over the floor! Police cars have been coming and going all morning."

"State trooper cars, Sheridan police cars, Terryville police cars, a crime scene investigation van, everybody and their uncle has been in and out of here," added another lady, sipping from a Buzz Coffee shop to-go mug.

"What happened? Was it an accident?" Sadie asked moving closer. A small gasp escaped her lips and her blue eyes widened in shock. My hand instinctively jumped to cover my mouth, disbelieving anything like that could happen in Alton Oaks.

"Must be an accident," said the woman. "There ain't been a murder in the history of Alton Oaks, best I can remember," she added. I rubbed away the goose bumps that collected on my arms as I looked towards the store for a clue that would confirm her story.

Our conversation was cut off by a short-lived hush that fell over the crowd as the paramedics wheeled a body bag into the ambulance. As soon as the doors shut, waves of muttering swept through the crowd like the wave at a baseball game. I watched while officials in various uniforms signed papers attached to clipboards, took notes, and exchanged information on the outside of the vehicle.

"Do you think it's true?" Sadie muttered as we watched the scene unfold.

Living in Albuquerque was different than life in

Alton Oaks; stuff like this was always on the news. This was the kind of thing that only happened in Chicago or Davenport, not our little town. "I guess it's possible," I replied, letting the possibility of this corruption sink in.

As the ambulance turned west on Oak, towards St. Collette's Hospital, the crowd began to thin. As locals made their way to work or their standard morning appointments at The Buzz, three uniformed officers exited the store. I immediately recognized Sheriff Gomes, with his head of white hair that climbed down to a beard and his round belly—the children of Alton Oaks often thought he was Santa Claus.

The second officer was a tall, brunette woman, wearing a blue Sheridan deputy's uniform. I recognized her as Beth Foster, someone I knew who went to high school with my brother because she was on the basketball team too.

The third officer was familiar. It took a few moments to register. "Is that Jake?" I asked Sadie in a low voice and sunk my head to her level like it was a secret.

Sadie's head jerked up from a conversation she was eavesdropping on, to where the officers were gathered. "Yeah," she said passively. "He became the town deputy about a year ago." Sadie then moved closer to the two mothers pushing strollers, standing a few feet away, and continued to eavesdrop.

As I watched him refer to a small Steno pad, I tried to decipher his features like a secret code. When I finally was able to recognize him as the same boy I'd lived down the street from, nostalgia hit me like a wrecking ball. He and Sadie had been my best friends in grade school. She and I grew apart from Jake in middle school... and I might have had a tiny crush on Jake Vega in high school, but only for a short period.

After puberty, he became talented at melting into the shadows and I went from looking forward to our morning niceties at the bus stop to forgetting he was there when volleyball, driver's ed, SATs, and college applications overshadowed him.

He used to have dirty blonde hair that was long enough to curl at its ends and would drape in front of his eyes during gym class. Now he had a short Captain America haircut which made his brown eyes seem more intense and focused. He wasn't much taller than I remembered, which kept him under six foot, nearly eye-to-eye with me.

Jake closed his Steno pad and shook Beth's hand authoritatively. As he made his way to the sheriff's old-fashioned station wagon, our eyes met. My first instinct was to look away, but I was still studying what was different about him and looked away later than I should have. His eyes were full of confidence and determination, just like his gait. It was like a Jake from *Twilight Zone*.

Sadie glanced at her phone for the time. Turning to me she said, "Oh, booger butts!" and stomped her leg. Sadie found the use of G-rated interjections hilarious and used them often. While working in the pediatric ward, I'm sure she had to watch her mouth. "I've gotta go. I'll take a rain check on the coffee, but text me as soon as you hear *anything* about what happened." She knew my mom would have gathered the whole story long before the clock struck noon.

"You got it," I said and watched her walk past her apartment building where her truck was parked somewhere on First Street West. She had waved to people I'm sure she saw each morning as she left for work.

Alone in the dissipating crowd, I suddenly felt alienated in a world I used to know. Sadie seemed to have it all together and, being an Alton by blood, I felt more out of place than ever when I couldn't recognize one stranger around me. This was not my life or my morning routine. A small stabbing pain of panic arose when self-doubting questions swelled in me like a tidal wave. Once again, I let the pooling tears in my eyes dry before they could drop, and swallowed the anxiety before it got out of control. Just then a crisp morning breeze tore through my hoodie and sweatpants which nudged me in the direction to return home for a hot shower.

As I walked past the grocers, I watched Jim Browski through the window of Prescott's, whose closed sign still hung on the door. He stood across from his wife, Tammy, who held their two-year-old son as he struggled to escape from her arms. I found it odd that a toddler was at a crime scene, but I guess no one really plans to hire babysitters for unexpected tragedies, especially so early in the morning.

Jim had on a flannel shirt and dirty jeans— something more fitting to wear on a camping trip than to his job as store manager. He looked defeated as he shrugged his shoulders to his wife's muted questions and ran a hand through his thinning hair in disbelief at what had happened.

"Charli Parker." A voice punctured the air like a crack in the sidewalk that checks your balance. My head spun to the curb where Jake stood beside the station wagon, his arms crossed over his chest and his green-tinted aviators covered his eyes. The brown lines on his khaki uniform pants made him seem taller than he was.

He uncrossed his arms and stepped up onto the curb. "Is it true? Has Charli Parker finally returned home?" He let out a small chuckle as he took off his sunglasses and studied my expression. "You look good, kid," he added.

This was a different Jake Vega than the one I'd known in high school; one who spewed confidence—a personality even. It took a while for my brain to register that this man was the same guy from my teenage memories. "You remember me, don't you?" he finally asked after words had failed me.

Snapping out of it, I said, "Yeah, sorry, Jake. I'm back. I forgot how quickly news spreads in this town." A few bicyclists cycled past and Jake's attention briefly went to them. I assumed he was making sure they were following the town's bicycling laws. It gave me a chance to study his profile and notice that he grew into his nose, though there was a small bump near the top where he'd broken it playing dodgeball in third grade.

Returning his gaze towards me, he nodded with a smile. The broad rimmed deputy hat briefly cast a shadow on the brick wall beside us at the movement. "How was Arizona?" he asked.

"New Mexico," I corrected him as two women pushing strollers brushed past us.

"My apologies," he said, briefly touching the brim of his hat with a nod. "What brings you back?"

I found this conversation strange because I couldn't place his tone. Was he treating me like a witness, a suspect, or just being more friendly than I expected? He was talking to me like we'd kept in touch after high school and I couldn't help but think his interest had an ulterior motive. However, I couldn't stop thinking about the grade school friendship we had, which kept me from ending the conversation. "Long story," I replied with a sigh, hoping he wouldn't ask more about it. I looked towards the hardware store across the street, trying to think of a question that would change the subject.

Jake beat me to it, though, and nodded to the

Prescott's grocery bag in my hand that held my mother's fruit. "Did Jim open the store already?" he asked.

We both knew he didn't, but I let him lead the conversation to another place. "Oh, no. Sadie and I went last night," I informed him, lifting the bag and letting it drop back to my side, the plastic crinkling against my sweat pants.

Reaching for the Steno pad inside his jacket, he asked, "What time was that?" Flipping it open, he reviewed his notes, waiting for my answer.

I replayed the night in my head and finally responded with, "Just after dark. The sun had just set, so maybe 7:30ish?"

Jake's wide-brimmed hat moved with his nod. "Did you notice anything out of the ordinary? Someone unfamiliar? Was Sara acting strange?" His gaze was hard and focused on answers.

I sighed and shrugged. "I don't know, Jake. Everyone seems unfamiliar." I glanced at the people on the street and behind store front windows. Ten years ago I knew them all, but age and stress changed their faces. "Actually, she *was* bothered," I said, directing my eyes back to Jake. "Impatient. Annoyed. Unless that's how she always is." The sun was getting higher in the sky and peeked over the buildings. I had to squint to see Jake's reaction.

Jake didn't say anything, but jotted something down on his pad of paper. When he finally did look up, he pulled something out of his jacket. "If you remember anything else, be sure to give me a call," he said, handing me his card. "Or stop by the station," he added, tucking the Steno pad back into his jacket. "We could use all the help we can get," he added under his breath.

I nodded, studying the embossed print and placed the card into my sweater pocket. Turning, I took a few steps to leave, ready to spend the entire walk home dissecting the conversation, until Jake said over a passing breeze, "It's great seeing you again, Charli," his hand on the door of the station wagon. "Welcome home." He smiled and I felt a rush of goose bumps that were different from the ones the morning chill had delivered.

I unwilling pulled my cheeks into a forced smile. "Thanks, Jake," I replied and picked up the pace to put as much distance between us as I could. It wasn't that I didn't trust him, but I think, given the opportunity, I would trust him too much.

CHAPTER 5

As I walked past the junior high and elementary schools, there were a lot of parents standing around and talking about the events of the morning. Not wanting to stop and chat with forgotten faces from high school, I avoided eye contact and sprinted up Oak Street until the spaces between houses became larger and the cemetery disappeared into the oak trees. It was then I could see the Alton house clearly at the end of the street.

My mother sat on the porch swing with my sister Bailey, while Mrs. Kratsky sat on the rocking chair in her hand-knitted sweater and slip-on shoes. Each gripped a hot beverage in their hands as steam billowed from the top of each rim.

"Charli Parker!" Mrs. Kratsky gasped with her hands raised in excitement. She rose from the wooden rocker smoothly as if her seventy-year old bones weren't aging at all. She looked like a kindly old woman, but she was a firecracker with a lot of spunk. "Look at you, grown into an adult while you've been away!"

She embraced me in a rib-cracking hug that smelled of fresh baked bread and moth balls. I always thought of Mrs. Kratsky as my grandmother. As a child she would babysit my siblings and me, and she would sneak us chocolate and ice cream bars when we played outside. "Looks can be deceiving," I replied, giving her a grin as I pulled away.

My younger sister, Bailey, sat stoically beside my mother. For as long as I could remember I could always find her next to my mother. She was her baby—even adopting my mother's shorter stature and blonde hair (unlike my brother and me) that made them look like a natural pair. I sighed with the frustration and comfort the scene gave me. Since Bailey lived next door to my mother now, she would unintentionally make me feel like I was the younger sister who knew nothing about my mother's life whenever I came to visit.

And this morning, Bailey looked incredibly comfortable in gray wool leggings, cozy boots, and an oversized sweatshirt that clung to her petite frame. Her long blonde hair was in a braid that hung over her shoulder. One leg was tucked under her and the other lazily pushed the porch swing from the floor. *My sister could make the grubbiest clothes look fashionable*, I thought as I thumbed the hole in the seam of my sweatpants. I sighed. "Hey, Bailey," I greeted, nodding in her direction.

"Hey, Charli," she cooed and smiled affectionately. Her gaze immediately drifted down to the spoon that stirred the coffee in her mug.

Handing my mother her bag of frozen strawberries, I noticed how quiet the porch had gotten. I assumed everyone was avoiding the elephant in the room: my abrupt and solo return to Alton Oaks. Trying to keep the conversation light, I asked, "Where's my adorable nephew?" I had only seen Eli a few times since his birth; he didn't really know me. I think I might have made an impression on him when I sent him a children's drum kit for his last birthday, but I hadn't seen him since Christmas before last.

Bailey lifted her perfectly plucked eyebrows in my direction. "He's with Carter. They're doing some man-themed thing today in Knox County. Turkey hunting or something," she shared, waving her hand like it wasn't important.

My sister had married her high school boyfriend

when she was nineteen and immediately had Eli. My nephew was a bundle of four-year-old energy that kept my sister on her toes. When her husband had his days off as a fireman, she basked in the hours when she could put herself first, instead of Eli. *Even Bailey could do the marriage thing right*, I admitted sourly to myself, letting my shoulders slump, then immediately tried to erase the thought.

That familiar rusty sound of the springs on the screen door made me turn to see my dad coming out of the house. He was dressed in a white shirt and tie, ready to go to work. My face lit up; he was my favorite person. "Daddy!" I exclaimed, turning to greet him.

"Charlotte May I?!" The animation in my dad's voice made my smile grow larger. He'd given me that nickname years ago because he would play *Mother May I?* with me as a bedtime game when I was younger. "Charlotte, may I take two steps forward? Charlotte, may I check your breath to be sure you brushed your teeth? Charlotte, may I read a bedtime story?" I loved those games. My older brother would sometimes call me Charli May I, but usually before giving me a noogie.

Dad's arms opened wide for a hug and I ran into them; his arms would always mean home to me. He either smelled like a bar of soap or the kitchen of Oakies. Today it was a meadow-fresh scent. "It's been too long since you visited, Charli," he said, picking me up slightly in his hug. When he let go, he spun me in a circle like a dancer. "Look at you, little Charlotte May. Promise me you'll come to Oakies for dinner tonight? I'll have Oscar make you his special breaded steak sandwich."

"I can't say no to Oscar's breaded steak! Seven o'clock?" I asked.

He picked up his accordion folder of papers that he'd

tossed to the floor in exchange for the hug. "Better make it eight," he said, kissing my forehead. "I've gotta head out."

Bending over, he gave my mom a kiss on her head, and then did the same to Bailey. My mother only pursed her lips together in disapproval at him, but he didn't catch it. I know she hated the attention he gave me and repeatedly wished he'd do the same for Bailey, but Bailey and my mother got along like peanut butter and jelly. My dad liked to go fishing and hunting and hiking and camping—things Bailey did not like. He tried to spend time with her, but they never had anything in common. It didn't mean he loved her less and Bailey knew that; it was reiterated with every hug, kiss, visit, and conversation. But my mom was convinced that since he spent more time with me, he loved Bailey less.

I watched my dad pull his bike from the driveway, put his belongings in the basket, and cycle down Oak. "So, Charli, what did you see when you passed Prescott's this morning?" my mother asked and took a sip of coffee. I took a cleansing breath and mentally prepared myself before turning to face the crowd of women on the porch: let the questioning begin (as long as it was not about my marriage).

It didn't surprise me that my mother had heard the news about Sara already, but that didn't stop me from asking, "How did you find out already?" She took it as a compliment that she didn't have to leave her house in order to be up-to-date on town happenings.

"Darren, the paper boy, told me when I returned from my morning walk in the cemetery," Mom mentioned and picked a ball of lint from her sweater. She sounded proud of herself for having that connection.

"Frannie called me," Mrs. Kratsky interjected, taking

a sip of coffee as a slight breeze ruffled her grey-streaked hair. "She was taking the kids to school and called me as soon as she got home. To get the full story, I came to see your mom." Mrs. Kratsky nodded at my mother in recognition.

Bailey leaned forward, the morning light highlighted the sun-kissed streaks in her hair, and she asked, "So what did you see? What happened? Weren't you there last night?" Her thin eyebrows rose and disappeared behind her side-swept bangs with her words.

I shrugged and sat on my hands to warm them from the morning chill. I didn't know what new information I could offer. "Apparently an employee was killed—Sara something."

All eyes were on me, but Bailey was the one who pushed for more information. "Well, didn't you see anything when you were there last night?"

I sighed, tired of having the attention on me. My eyes slid over the oak trees in the front yard as I thought about last night's events. "Well, Sara checked us out at the register, at least that's what her name tag said—"

"You think there was foul play? That name tags were switched? That it wasn't really Sara?" Bailey's tone rose at the possible scandal.

My eyebrows furrowed at how excited my sister got at the prospect of corrupt activity. I tried not to roll my eyes as I stated, "Bailey, it's Alton Oaks. Get real."

Her features dipped. "It's entirely possible," she said, being sure to pronounce each word to barely hide her sour disposition. Then she turned up her nose, leaned back against the green pillows on the porch swing and blew the hair that had fallen in her face.

I momentarily felt bad for putting her out, but before I could address it, my mother asked, "What else, Charli?" Her eyes were hungry for a first hand account.

"Nothing really. She was upset—more irritated." I

fiddled with my hands, still uneasy with the attention I was getting.

"Was there anyone else in the store? Did you see anyone?" Mrs. Kratsky offered. Her legs were crossed and her slip-on shoe was balancing on her toe as she gently wiggled her foot back and forth.

"No, the store was pretty empty." I looked down at my shoes thinking about it. "Oh!" I exclaimed and jumped slightly due to a revelation, causing the other women to do the same. "Earlier when I was meeting Sadie on the corner, I saw her arguing with a guy. He was about her age: about this tall." I put a hand up indicating his height, "and he wore a Cubs jersey."

"Oh, that's probably her boyfriend, Calvin," my mom offered. "He was always hanging around the store when she was working. His mom is Carla, Jenna's best friend. Remember her, Charli?" I nodded briefly so my mother could continue. My cousin, Jenna, and Carla had been inseparable when they were younger. Carla was always at family get-togethers and, since they were ten years older than us, would babysit us on occasion. The last time I saw Calvin was at my sister's wedding six years ago, but it still shocked me that I didn't recognize him.

My mother continued, "I heard he was offered an academic scholarship to Chicago State in the fall. I honestly don't know why they were a couple; he could do so much better. Sara always seemed to be bossing him around and didn't like him to have a life outside of her. I don't know why he put up with her."

"Maybe he couldn't take it anymore and he let her have it," Bailey said, leaning forward and raising her eyebrows with the speculation.

"I doubt it, honey," my mom said, tapping Bailey's knee reassuringly.

Bailey once again leaned back in the swing, proud to

share the information she was about to offer. "Well, *I* heard Sara was in love with Jim."

I laughed a bit too loudly at this information. Jim, the store manager of Prescott's, was average in high school. Now his hair was thinning—what he had looked like cotton candy—and his stomach was getting plumper. You couldn't pick him out of a crowd. He was so ordinary. "Sorry," I apologized when Bailey shot me a look of disdain. "I know I haven't been around much, but that's a bit hard to swallow."

"I never heard about that!" My mother was taken aback with this information and turned to fully face my sister. Bailey drank in the attention. "Where did you hear that from? Why didn't you tell me?" my mother questioned further.

"Some of the pre-school moms get together on Wednesdays for coffee and it's a huge gossip-fest. Wendy—Sara's cousin—let it slip after too much 'creamer' in her coffee." Bailey used air quotes to emphasize she meant liquor instead of creamer and went back to stirring her coffee with a spoon.

My mother, shocked to hear this, started showering Bailey with questions as Mrs. Kratsky silently observed, the rocking chair she sat in creaking on the aged wooden floorboards.

As everyone got more and more animated, the sound of a motorcycle sliced through the conversation. All of our heads turned towards the street, expecting it to be another out-of-town Canary who'd missed the turn onto US-16. To our surprise, though, the motorcycle pulled into the driveway of the empty house just a few acres away. Jaws hung open when we could just see the motorist pause at the front door and then walk inside.

"What is happening? Who is that?" Mrs. Kratsky asked, squinting into the distance. I wondered if she could see as much of the scene as we could without a pair of glasses. I turned to my mother whose hand grasped the pendant on her necklace—a nervous habit she'd always had. And, for the first time, my mother had no answer.

"Excuse me," my mother said, picking up her frozen strawberries, pulling out her cell phone, and disappearing into the house.

"I think I'm going to head downtown to get more coffee," Bailey said, rising from the swing and dashing down the stairs. Bailey got all of her good gossip from The Buzz and today it would actually be buzzing with the talk of the town.

I had to leave too. I had to go to the police station to see Jake.

That motorcycle... I'd seen it before.

CHAPTER 6

Mrs. Kratsky hopped into her golf cart and, presumably, made her way into town. As I descended the stairs, my mind reeling over information I'd forgotten about last night, I stopped when the ragged bottom of my ten-year old sweatpants caught on the splintering wood of the stairs. A few birds cawed as they flew overhead and I decided that changing into more presentable clothes would be a good idea before I set out to the historic downtown part of Alton Oaks.

Upstairs in my quiet bedroom, I pulled my suitcase from where I'd placed it maybe twenty-four hours ago. As I unzipped it, the scent of my Albuquerque apartment—dollar store grade plug-in air fresheners and a hint of Jackson's stale cigarette smoke—knocked me over with nostalgia. I fought the urge to reminisce over such memories because I had something more important to do. I pushed aside the guilt, frustration, and sadness to pull out a pair of jeans and a cotton shirt that still tried to plague me with flashbacks of my former life.

The house was empty when I descended the stairs— my mother was no longer sitting in the kitchen talking into her cell phone. Walking through the front door, I made to lock the door behind me—a habit I'd built up living in Albuquerque—and, with a smile, realized I was in Alton Oaks. I wasn't even sure if we still had keys to our doors. This awareness helped fight away the memories that threatened to spill each time I caught a whiff of Jackson on my shirt.

Walking only on the weathered and somewhat mossy stepping-stones beside the house—a childhood habit—I made my way to the garage to find a bicycle. I knew I would run into a slew of people on my way to the police station on the south end of Main Street. Everyone would be out looking for information, and since I was back in town I knew I would be stopped several times by people I hardly knew anymore with questions I didn't want to answer. If I rode my bike down the bike path along the canal instead, I could count on a lot fewer interactions.

The garage was borderline dilapidated, but still housed plastic storage containers, rusted yard equipment, and old childhood toys that should have been evicted years ago. After battling a forest of cobwebs in the dank, dark space, jumping from the rustling of frightened animals, and using the light that filtered in through the holes in the roof, I found my old purple road bike wedged between a tool chest and my grandmother's 1950-era silver Christmas tree. Struggling with the flat tires and rusty gears, I pulled it from the shadows and let it rest against the side of the house. I made a mental note to see if Mr. Kratsky could bring it back to its glory.

Mom's bike was in pristine condition despite its near constant use. After adjusting the seat, I hopped on and made my bumpy way down Oak Street. I thought she wouldn't mind lending it to me since it was her day off off work at the library and that she was mysteriously already out of the house. (Where in the world did she go?) As I hopped on and began peddling down Oak, it occurred to me that I couldn't remember the last time I'd ridden a bike other than the three months when I avidly participated in a cycling class at the local gym. It was a way for me to work through the stress and anxiety of Jackson's emotional distance and the frequency with which he was coming home at odd hours in the night. I never asked him where he'd been or what he was doing because I was always afraid of the answer.

By now, the sun had warmed the town, but as I whipped through the air, I wished I'd been wearing a pair of gloves. As Oak Street transformed from a dirt and gravel road to smooth pavement, I pulled the sleeves of my sweater over my freezing cold knuckles, still gripping the handlebars. Cutting through the Kratsky's empty backyard and the school parking lots, I rode on the dirt trail that generations of Alton Oaks' kids used to access the Canal Trail. It was refreshing to see that even though we lived in a world of electronic entertainment, today's Alton Oaks kids did not let the trail grow over.

All too often people take their home for granted. I had been so preoccupied with escaping it in my past, I couldn't truly see how beautiful my hometown could be. When I'd left at eighteen, I struggled with who I was and who I wanted to become. I put a negative spin on everything because I knew I couldn't grow here. I was lost in my little sister's perfect shadow and ignored by my bright, charming and talented older brother.

When the branches that hovered over the dirt trail opened and spilled onto the perfectly maintained and paved path, the reflection of the sun greeted me on the river. As I switched gears and picked up speed, I let the air wash my face from this morning's drama. Closing my eyes for a moment, I took a deep breath of nature's sweet scent. The crisp aroma of the river was cleansing; that dank, slightly fishy, mineral smell that reminded me of summers tubing down the river, or fishing on Sunday mornings with Dad. The few boats that were on the river left a wake which traveled to the rocky shore just a few feet from the path where the young cattails bowed and spiders crept on water-specked webs. The sun glimmered like stars on the water and I made a mental note to spend some time out here with my camera.

It was a normal hometown scene: serious and leisurely bicyclists were on the road for their morning bout of exercise, retired men were fishing while sitting on folding chairs or coolers full of beer, moms were walking their children in strollers and the occasional jogger would whiz past lost in the rhythm of their pace, sometimes the beats from their earbuds would trail behind them in the breeze.

When I reached the Town Circle—a cul de sac of government buildings on the south end of our historic downtown—I parked the bike in the closest bicycle rack and walked down Main Street into the heavy double doors of the police station.

It was small and cramped inside, with too many bodies mulling about. There were two men behind the desk talking over a manila file folder. Immediately, I recognized one of them as Seth Granger, Sadie's boyfriend from the tenth grade. "Charli Parker!" His face lit up as he waved the other man away and came closer so that his thighs just grazed the papers on the desk between us. "I haven't seen you in years! How are you?" His hands rested on his hips which was loaded with a belt of tools, including a gun, as he smiled at me.

"I'm good, Seth." I suddenly missed the anonymity of being in Albuquerque. Nevertheless, I put on a smile and played along. "How are you?" I asked, hoping the topic would stay on him.

"Doin' great!" He was in a good mood despite the chaos that had descended upon our town and, of course, our police department. "Susan and I have three kids now. Seven, four, and an eight-month old. How about you? Heard you got married a while ago."

This was exactly the topic I wanted to avoid. Admitting my marriage was over made me feel like a failure—what had I done with my life? I didn't want people to see me as my mistakes. "Yeah, hey, is Jake around? I need to talk to him."

Seth briefly looked around the room and replied, "He's been busy with what happened at Prescott's this morning. I could take a message and make sure he gets it." His hands moved over the cluttered desk looking for a pen.

I bit my lip at this. "Actually, I wanted to talk to him about that. I remembered something I saw last night."

Just as Seth was about to reply, Jake walked around the corner with a handful of papers. He handed them to Seth who adopted a more serious attitude and went straight to the phone. "Couldn't stay away, could you, Charli?" Jake asked and smiled like he knew a secret I wasn't privy to yet.

My cheeks grew warm and I avoided meeting his eyes, embarrassed by my reaction. "I actually wanted to talk to you about something I remembered last night at Prescott's."

The smile faded from his face as he went into police-mode. Jake reached down to unlatch the short wooden swing-door that kept civilians from wandering too deep into the station. "Come with me and we'll find a place to talk," he said, motioning for me to come around the desk.

It was warm inside the station and I unzipped my sweater as I followed Jake's lean figure through a maze of desks and bodies. Phones were ringing, metal drawers of filing cabinets opened and closed, and too many conversations were happening at once.

Jake ended up taking me to a desk at the far end of the police station where the volume was only slightly lower. I sat in an uncomfortable wooden chair beside a metal desk, where he sat down and pulled out his Steno pad. "I don't remember there being this many police on the Alton Oaks police force," I said a little overwhelmed.

Jake shook his head. "We just have a lot of people in to help out with the crime scene and investigation."

"Crime scene? So it's true? It wasn't an accident?" I asked and then realized I was acting like my mother. Promptly, I relaxed my features and sat back, trying not to look too eager to hear his answer.

Jake's eyes searched mine while he obediently kept his lips from flapping. "I can't say until we get the autopsy report, Charli." His lips moved to form another sentence but stopped. It seemed as if there was more he wanted to share but couldn't and I pushed down that Alton-nosiness that arose in me to ask more questions.

Ultimately, I nodded, understanding his predicament. It was a bit refreshing to talk to someone from Alton Oaks who wasn't willing to gossip. "Well I won't be long," I started, blowing the overgrown bangs from my face and fidgeting with my hands. "I just remembered something from last night. I don't know if it's important or not, but I figured it's better to say something than nothing at all." I hesitated and glanced at him. He watched me intently, probably weighing whether or not I was a credible source.

"A bit before we went into Prescott's," I continued, staring at his chest pocket where his badge gleamed in the light from his desk lamp. "I was waiting on the corner of Oak & Main for Sadie. I saw Sara arguing with a boy about her age near the back door. He was wearing jeans and a Cubs jersey. It might have been her boyfriend, Calvin, but I don't know."

As I rambled, Jake nodded, looking at the notes he'd jotted in his Steno pad. "Then later—I don't remember exactly when—maybe eight-thirty? Nine o'clock?—

Sadie and I were walking home from Froz T's and cut through the Prescott parking lot and we saw Sara with an older guy—he was maybe in his late twenties or early thirties—I'm not too sure. It was dark, but they were under the security light. He had short dark hair—and they were smoking by the back door." I looked up at the drop-ceiling panels above us to search my brain for more details, but none came.

Jake looked up, interested in this piece of information. His eyebrow rose slightly as he asked, "And you don't know who the guy is?"

Shaking my head, I looked from him to his Steno pad and replied, "No, but I didn't recognize Calvin either and I've known him since he was born. Everyone here looks different to me." I felt like I was getting off on a tangent and scolded myself. It was either the crowded police station that was making me nervous or it was Jake. I think he expected us to be friends again as easily as we were as children, but there was too big of a hiatus for that. Licking my lips, I added, "Well, Sadie didn't know him either and I think she knows nearly everyone in town. But, anyway, my point is I think I just saw him."

"And where was that?" Jake asked, looking up again from his notes, his eyes searching my face for a clue.

The temperature in the police station began to form beads of sweat on my temples and my lower back which was making me uncomfortable. "Remember that empty house across the street from your parents' house?" I asked, leaning forward.

Jake nodded and I continued, "I'm pretty sure I just watched him walk inside about half an hour ago."

"And why do you think it was him?" Jake lifted an eyebrow, glancing at me from his notes. He sat back in his chair, seemingly unimpressed with this information.

An officer briskly walked by Jake's desk, sending a

small breeze towards us and I let it temporarily relieve my perspiration. After taking a deep breath, I looked Jake in the eye and said, "He was wearing the same worn black leather jacket and he was riding a motorcycle, and the man at Prescott's last night was leaning on a motorcycle. It could be him." I couldn't read Jake's expression, but I suddenly felt like I was overreacting and maybe this information wasn't important to the case at all.

Jake tapped his pen on the pad of paper a few times, thinking. Finally, he said, "Thanks, Charli," and stood. As I followed suit, he added, "I'll look into this and see if it helps the case."

I smiled in response, and for a few moments I felt that old connection with him that we'd had in fourth grade, made of friendship—being on the same frequency with each other. Only this time instead of pretending to be Power Rangers in his front yard and fighting evil, we were two adults helping to figure out what was happing to our hometown.

Maybe I wasn't overreacting at all.

CHAPTER 7

I went home and took a nap.

Normally, Albuquerque-Charli doesn't sleep and doesn't nap. Albuquerque-Charli constantly tells herself there are more lessons to plan, or a project to outline, or laundry to do—that there's no room for sleep. But Alton Oaks-Charli did not feel one ounce of guilt as she walked into her old bedroom, fell onto her faded quilt, and quickly started snoozing.

I'm not one for remembering my dreams or interpreting them either (unlike Sadie). But once in a while I'd wake from a dream that was so intense it left me breathless or sweating from a fear whose claws were scraping slowly and silently away, leaving a trail of chilly trepidation. Those were difficult to ignore and they often haunted the empty moments of my day.

That afternoon I dreamt I was forced to live in a colony underwater, but I couldn't hold my breath very long. I discovered that if I breathed out of a tiny corner of my mouth when no one was looking, I could survive without breaching the surface. And no one was allowed to breach the surface. When I woke up, I sat in bed and focused on my breathing. At first, I was confused that it wasn't the orange-tinted bedroom I usually awoke alone in in Albuquerque. When I regained my senses and realized I was in Alton Oaks, I slowly sat up in the dying afternoon light.

With fading images of the dream still draped around me, I decided to get out of the house, and left early to make my way into town to have dinner with my father.

My mother was still absent, so I left a dark, empty house, with strong cold-air fueled drafts rifling through the plastic canvas and the wind whistling through the nooks and crannies. Shivering, I grabbed a flannel-lined jacket from the hall closet and let the screen door slam behind me in the porch light as I hopped down the stairs and into the driveway.

The breeze had grown a frigid coating, but I was glad I'd decided to walk instead of bike; I warmed up nicely in no time as I picked up my pace. This late at night our side of town was pretty desolate, unless there was something going on at the school. Stars littered the sky here on cloudless nights.

After I crossed the slight fork in the road that led to Highway 16, I found myself walking past the cemetery. Normally, I didn't walk on the north side of the street because it didn't have a sidewalk like the south side did, but I found the scenery calming despite the recent death in town and the fading memories of Netflix-induced horror that Sadie and I had indulged in the other night. No one was ever in a rush at the cemetery and there was always an aura of revered silence that even the animals adhered to.

Just past the junior high school, as I approached Sheridan Avenue, Carla crossed my path walking up Oak Street, underneath the street lights. Hanging from her right hand was a white plastic Prescott's grocery bag, and I assumed she was on her way home. She looked distracted and barely noticed me until I had said something.

"Hi, Carla." I had stopped on the corner and her head snapped up from looking down at the shadowy sidewalk.

"Oh, hi, Charli. I heard you were back in town." She gave me a weak hug and it seemed like it took a lot of energy for her to give pleasantries.

"I am. How are you doing? How's Calvin? My mom told me he was close to Sara. Do you need anything?" I honestly didn't want to come across as intrusive or fishing for gossip; Carla looked so caught up in her thoughts that I wanted to offer my help. After all, she was practically my cousin, too.

Carla shrugged. Her short, dark, curly hair momentarily touched her shoulders with the movement, and she forced a half smile. "Oh no, thank you, Charli. Cal's pretty beat up about it. He and Sara had been dating since sophomore year. The police had him in for questioning this morning." She sighed, looking past me, and added, "I just don't understand it."

I nodded, seeing that there was more Carla wanted to say. The wind picked up for a moment, making our hair dance beyond our shoulders. The shadows beneath the lamp lights danced frantically like teenagers.

Carla secured her navy blue plastic headband and, with tired eyes, she continued, "Cal is such a bright young man. I know I'm biased because I'm his mother, but he couldn't have done it and it hurts that he's even a suspect." Pain deepened the creases around her eyes. She continued to look at me instead of the scenery around us and added, "Did you know he was offered a scholarship to Chicago State? That's such a hard school to get into. He was so proud of himself—*I'm* so proud of him. That's why he went to Prescott's last night: he told Sara the news, only she wasn't happy about it. Sometimes she could be so selfish. She didn't want Cal to leave her behind and they had a big fight about it."

I bit my lip, sympathizing. Things were beginning to make sense, only Sara was not coming across as an innocent victim. She was beginning to come across as callous, with how people spoke of her. I reminded myself to stay open-minded.

Carla ran a hand through her hair. "Cal couldn't

have done it, Charli. It's not in him. And he took Oliver to the movies last night—" Her voice softened as she continued, "He's ten years old now, can you believe it?"

I smiled. I remembered the day Calvin became a big brother and he always treated it like a grand position, spoiling Oliver whenever he could. "Oh, now I feel old," I joked. "It seems like I last saw him when he was four."

Carla smiled, but it quickly faded. "I'm sorry for unloading all of this on you. I just really needed to vent to someone."

"Don't be sorry," I said, waving a dismissive hand. "I'm always available. I'm heading to Oakies for dinner; do you want to tag along, or would you like me to bring you something? I hear Oscar's chocolate lava cake relieves stress magnificently."

Carla smiled once more and it lingered a bit longer than the last. "No. Thank you though, Charli. Oliver's heart is set on French fries and chicken nuggets," she said, holding up the plastic grocery bag, letting it crinkle in the breeze.

"Only if you're sure," I said, giving her another hug.

Carla nodded, avoiding making eye contact.

"Everything's going to turn out fine," I encouraged. "Call me if you need anything, okay?"

"Thanks, Charli," Carla said with a limp smile as she began inching away. "If you see Jenna before I do, tell her Oliver loved the telescope."

I waved in acknowledgement and watched her walk away with a smile that I hoped showed support and encouragement instead of false interest. For the remainder of my walk I avoided eye contact with other pedestrians, which wasn't hard considering my mind was focused on the details of Carla's conversation and avoiding the violent gusts of wind.

Oakies Bar & Grill hadn't changed a bit and I liked that. The green and white neon sign stood out among the street lights and florescent lights of the surrounding stores. There were modern glass doors to pull open on the outside with window decals advertising current specials. Inside, there was a short hallway that housed bulletin boards with community information, chalkboards that detailed the upcoming events at Oakies, and twenty-five cent candy machines. Once you opened the wooden doors—which were the original entrance to the restaurant established in 1946—scents that made your tummy rumble wafted through the air at you and, like a magnet, pulled you deeper inside.

The walls were covered in old movie posters. The first four feet, from the ground up, were tiles decorated by generations of children that bordered the walls around the restaurant. The setting looked like a normal family restaurant with booths and tables. There was a set of stairs to the left of the entrance which descended to the bar with two large televisions mounted on the walls and, on Thursday nights, had live entertainment.

There were a few families in the restaurant, but the dinner rush was clearly over. The hostess behind the small table was on the phone and put a finger up to indicate she'd be right with me. Her drastically dark-haired bob bounced as she moved the phone to her other shoulder and shifted through the pages in front of her.

Looking around, I was surprised at how many faces I didn't immediately recognize. When we were younger we ate dinner here often and we knew all the wait staff. Now, though, the faces behind the aprons were much too young.

My dad walked out from the kitchen with a plate of food. He delivered it to a table nearby and interacted with the children. A restaurant manager might not be a job people think highly of, but my dad loved it. He used to say that it wasn't a job because it didn't feel like work. I liked that about my father—he didn't care for titles or material success; he knew more about happiness than most people.

Just as the hostess hung up the phone, my dad arrived by my side with a hug. "Hey, Charli, you made it!" he said and released me from his kitchen-scented hug.

"Of course, I did," I said. "I'm not in the position to turn down free food."

He laughed. "And here I thought you came for the company. Stab your father in the heart, you do," he joked.

Before I could counter his claim, my dad introduced me to the hostess who'd just finished writing something in the appointment book in front of her. "Hey, Janet, this is my oldest daughter, Charli," Dad said as he opened the register and began thumbing through receipts.

She smiled. Her dark hair, white skin and unnaturally red lips made me think of Snow White. "Hey," she greeted with a curt nod. "I remember you from when you were in high school," she added.

"Oh?" I said, confused. She looked much younger than me.

She nodded and her lips curved gently into a humored grin. "You used to come to the elementary school and help out with the homework program."

As she talked, I thought back to the volunteer hours I'd completed for my honors classes—I had all but forgotten that. Janet let a small laugh escape her lips. "I was the first grader who threw fits in the corner whenever anyone mentioned numbers—or math in general."

My laugh matched hers as I remembered the little long-haired girl with the fiercest set of lungs. "Yes, I remember you. I take it you've overcome your fear of nickels and dimes?"

She chuckled, pushing her hair behind her ear. "Yes. Although, I'm a much better hostess than a waiter who brings change." The bell on the door behind me tinkled and Janet picked up a few menus before adding, "It was nice seeing you again, Charli," and met the new customers at the door.

"Well," my dad said, turning to face me, "Charlotte May I eat dinner with you?" he asked, closing the register drawer and picking up a menu from the hostess station.

Beaming at the warmth in his smile, his voice, and his gestures, I answered, "You may."

We were in the middle of eating breaded steak sandwiches with garlic roasted rosemary potatoes when my dad stopped dancing around the subject of my return. "Are you okay, Charlotte May?" he asked, putting down what was left of his sandwich and wiping his hands on a napkin.

I took a bite of my sandwich as I watched him fold his hands and place them on the table in front of him, his attention solely on me and my reply. I liked that he was deliberate with his actions that way, not multi-tasking or asking in passing. He always did that, whether it was about an exam I'd studied all night for, a challenging volleyball game, or a fight with one of my siblings. But I didn't like that his attention was on a topic I wasn't sure I was ready to speak to anyone about, particularly my father. *At least it's not my mother asking*, I thought to myself with relief.

Taking a sip of my diet coke, I let the carbonated bubbles pop around my tongue before I nodded. "I'm okay," I said after letting the cold drink slip down my throat.

Several seconds passed until it almost became awkward. My dad cleared his throat when enough time elapsed and he asked, "Charlotte May I ask you a question?" Sneaking a look at him through my overgrown bangs, I saw concern etched into his eyebrows. I wanted to say no and avoid this topic altogether, but he was my dad and I hated to see him worry. With a barely discernible nod, I allowed it. "Your mother told me you had a fight and wanted to leave him. You're not the type to give up so easy, Charli. What really happened?"

Bless my father. Most of my family didn't completely hide the fact that they weren't fond of Jackson—especially my brother—but my dad always gave people the benefit of the doubt.

As I tried to find the right sentences, I looked around at the left-over dinner-rush families surrounding us: the squirmy child coloring on his kid's menu, the group of three teenagers talking animatedly over their plates of fries, and the couple clearly on a date, sipping their sodas and smiling sheepishly at each other. I saw my retired sixth grade teacher in a booth at the far end of the restaurant eating pie with her husband, and my old Girl Scout troop leader, now with graying hair, sitting with whom I assumed were her young grandkids. This was not the place to divulge the truth.

"We had a fight. Over something," I paused trying to find the right word, "unsavory." I hesitated to go further and avoided looking my father directly in the eye. I fussed with the napkin on the table, repeatedly folding over and unfolding the corner.

At once, my dad asked, "Did he hurt you?" His voice became hard and protective—a tone that I'd rarely heard my father take on.

I shook my head, letting my hair fall over my shoulders and onto my face. We were both silent. I studied how the creamed corn ran into the potatoes on my plate and I scraped them apart with my fork, listening to the ambient sounds of families and clinking dinnerware, which seemed to get louder during the pause in our conversation. Loud cheers floated up from the stairwell due to the restaurant's weekly Trivia Night, temporarily pausing conversations as patrons looked towards the source of the sudden sound.

I sighed, knowing my father wasn't going to drop the topic without more information. "I just... I can't do it anymore, Dad. I can't keep living with his excuses. I just..." I bit my bottom lip and creased my forehead knowing the words I said weren't very well chosen.

My dad reached across the table and put his hand on mine. "Stay," he said and squeezed my hand, "as long as you need."

Finally, I looked up to meet his eyes and, to my relief, there was no judgment. My lips pulled into something resembling a grin. "Thank you," I replied softly, relieved that he didn't need the whole story or to fish for details like my mother would be sure to do.

CHAPTER 8

When I left the restaurant satiated, I was lost in thoughts about what my future would be. A blast of wind swung the door out of my hands as I left the warm, delicious air of Oakies. With some effort, I got the door closed and then fished out the hood of my sweater from beneath the jacket.

Would I stay in Alton Oaks? If I did, would I continue to live with my parents? How would I pay my bills? Should I go back to Albuquerque for a few days to tie up loose ends? Would I want to run into Jackson again? How would I earn money? Ugh, I needed to find a job. These thoughts multiplied, their weight added to my shoulders, nearly burying me in worry. Distracted, I didn't see Jake until I nearly walked into him on the corner of Oak and Main.

"Hey, Charli!" Jake greeted as he approached the corner. He was still in his uniform so I wasn't sure if he was still on duty or on his way home.

"Hey, Jake, long day?" I asked, glancing at my wristwatch, realizing it was nearly ten o'clock at night.

"The longest," he replied exasperatedly. "Are you heading home?" He nodded up Oak towards the Alton house that stood somewhere in the distance.

"Yeah, I just had dinner with my dad. Oakies hasn't changed a bit." I smiled, realizing I liked that. No one was on the streets this late and in this weather. I was suddenly glad for Jake as not only a distraction from my thoughts, but as a companion on this dark and violent night.

Jake matched my stride as we walked down the street. "Some people either love that about Oakies or hate it. I'm just glad the menu hasn't changed much; you can't mess with perfection."

I laughed at that. "I agree one hundred percent," I said with a smile, but our conversation quickly died. When a cold wind raced down the street, I zipped up my sweater and pulled the hood back over my head. Reaching my quota of awkward silences for the day, I dug my hands deeper into the front pockets of my sweater and quickly asked, "Hey, did you hear anything about that guy I told you about?"

Jake looked at me with a frown. "You know I can't discuss any information about an open case, especially in a town like ours."

I unconsciously sighed. "I understand." I forced a sympathetic smile. "I just was wondering if we should be worried about that stranger walking into an empty house so close to my parents. We're so far from town..." Okay, maybe I was fishing for information.

Jake scanned the street ahead of us, always alert. "He's new to town, just moved into that house. His name is," Jake paused for a moment to think, "Rip Oakley. And that's just town gossip, not relevant to the case." He winked good-humoredly before putting his hands into the faux sheep-skinned pockets of his brown deputy's jacket.

We walked a block or so in silence, with only the sound of a few cars on Sheridan Avenue and the serenade of crickets hiding in the grass.

"Well," Jake said, breaking the silence. "What do you plan on doing?"

I turned my body to face him as we kept walking, so that my hood didn't fall from my head. "What do you mean?" I asked, balling my fists and pushing them deeper into the pockets of my jacket, testing its seams.

His features were highlighted in the last of the street lights as we crossed the street. "Are you back in Alton Oaks to stay, or are you heading back to Arizona?"

"New Mexico," I corrected. Jake shrugged as if they were one and the same.

After a handful of quiet moments, he followed up his question with, "Well?"

Sighing with obvious agitation, I shrugged my shoulders. "I don't know, Jake. I have a liberal arts degree and spent the past four years teaching to English Language Learners. The only other experience I have is building sustainable farms in third world countries from my Peace Corps days... There isn't really a market for either in Alton Oaks. I have no idea what I'm going to do." My voice was hard and slightly aggressive with how nosy he was being.

"Maybe you're meant to do something else?" he asked. His voice was tentative, knowing he'd hit a nerve and was trying to be reassuring.

Rolling my eyes from beneath my hood, I asked haughtily, "Like what?"

With a tone of indifference, he replied, "Oh, I don't know. What did you enjoy doing when you weren't at work?"

I pictured myself sitting on the couch, grading papers, making lesson plans, and watching a movie while I constantly checked my cell phone for messages, wondering if my husband would come home that night. Stifling another sigh, and choking down the painful memories, my tone softened a bit and I hesitantly shared, "Well, I like taking photographs. Not professionally, but for friends and on road trips and stuff."

An RV with a loaded bicycle rack rumbled down the street in the hailing wind. We watched it climb Oak Street as we walked, until we barely saw its taillights disappear as it made the turn onto Highway 16. "Have you ever thought about doing that?" he asked. "You know, taking pictures for a living."

"No." It was a word that came out as incredulously as possible. That would not have been a stable career choice.

Jake put his hands up again, jokingly in defense, and the gesture softened my mood. "Just an idea," he explained with the hint of a smile. "The newspaper is always looking for freelance photographers at the big events. I doubt it pays much, if at all, but it's something."

Another block or so passed in silence as I thought about the possibility. There was a crescent moon high in the sky and the air seemed colder the further from town we traveled. The Kratsky's house was coming into view when I asked, "What about you, Jake?"

His hands were still inside the pockets of his uniform jacket when he turned his palms up to shrug. "What about me?"

"I haven't had a conversation with you like this since junior high. Fill in the blanks from then 'til now," I said, watching the television light flicker across the curtains in the Kratsky's living room window.

"Deflection," he stated simply with a smirk, knowing I was changing the subject. I gave him a playful nudge with my elbow so that he'd let me take the conversation down a different road. "Oh, I don't know," he began. "I was aimless in high school," he said with a shrug. "My parents sent me to college in Bloomington. I hated it there and joined the police academy without telling them."

"Jake Vega!" I exclaimed, shocked. "I would never have guessed you would be the type."

Growing up, Jake was always so straight-laced. He played by the rules, never missed curfew, and constantly sought his parents' approval for every decision—which was quite frustrating when ten-year-old Sadie and I wanted to sneak down to the cornfield on the other side of town, or go past our boundaries in the oak trees to play in the creek.

"We all have that bit of angsty rebellion in us once in a while," he admitted.

"How did your parents find out?" I asked, seeing the lights of the Alton House in the distance.

"I didn't hide it very well. They had their suspicions and drove down one weekend. They found out I was no longer in the dorms. My mother didn't talk to me for months. In the end, everything worked out, though. My parents retired and moved to California with my sister and her family."

"California?" I asked, impressed. "I thought she was in North Carolina."

Jake shook his head, his eyes squinting in the blast of wind that hurled down the street. "She went there for college, but then moved to California right about the time we graduated high school," he explained.

"I knew your old house looked different," I retorted. "Who lives there now?" It was the house next to Bailey's, and she'd never shared any gossip on that piece of information.

"*I* still do," he said smiling like it was common knowledge. We had just walked past the cemetery where Jake's property line began, although we were on the other side of the street. "What? You think I'm walking you home because I'm a gentleman?" he asked jokingly, poking me in the ribs.

My lips spread into a smile. "Oh, and here I was all a-flutter," I joked in a southern accent and waved my hand like it was a fan that kept me from fainting.

We laughed and stopped in front of Rip Oakley's dark and empty house just as another blast of wind shook through the trees. I cowered deeper into the hood around my head and held my breath as it passed. "I bought the house from my parents so they could retire in California. It's just me in that old house."

"Is it weird living in the house you grew up in?" I asked.

"You tell me," he said and his gaze went towards the Alton house.

"No," I said, stuttering. "That's different. It's still the house I grew up in. Everything is just like it was. *Everything*. It's not my house."

Jake's eyebrows rose and I felt flustered. Why was I getting so defensive?

"I don't think it's weird," he finally shared, his eyes moving from his feet to my face with a shrug. "It's not really my parents' house anymore. It's mine."

"Oh," I said and smiled, unsure of how to respond. Another gust of wind bit into us and I said, "I better go. Thanks for keeping me company, Jake."

Without hesitating, I gave him a hug. His warmth was inviting and his collar smelled like a nothing-special laundry detergent and the musk of something I couldn't place. It wasn't until I released him from the hug that I realized how awkward the gesture could have been. I was relieved to see that his smile said it wasn't. His hand lingered on my shoulder before he dropped it and confidently added, "It's good having you back in Alton Oaks, Charli."

"Thanks, Jake," I said and waved as he crossed the street to his house.

Stuffing my hands deeper into my sweater, I quickened my pace. Soon I passed my cousin Jenna's brightly-lit sidewalk and a few acres later, I climbed up the creaking stairs of my mother's house. My mood shifted suddenly from jovial to cautious. A shiver ran down my spine and as I reached for the doorknob I felt a pair of eyes on my back. Taking a quick glance into the dark landscape behind me, I heard an owl hooting and saw nothing but the shadows from an angry wind. Promptly, I scurried into the house, and felt silly when I made sure I locked the door behind me.

CHAPTER 9

"So, how was your first forty-eight hours back home?" Sadie asked as we took a shortcut through the cemetery the next day, on our way to Prescott's for groceries. We had met up for coffee in the morning and were walking down Main and up the Canal Trail since it was such a lovely spring morning, despite the howling wind I'd barely slept through the night before.

"Well, at least my homecoming isn't on the top of the gossiping list," I admitted.

"No kidding!" she exclaimed. "First you come back, then there's a dead body at the grocery store, and now a reclusive sexy stranger has moved into the house that's been vacant for as long as I can remember. You chose an excellent time to come home." As Sadie talked, the long silver necklace she wore swung against her pale pink shirt as if it was nodding, agreeing to everything she was saying.

I laughed; Sadie could always make me smile. Even from halfway across the country, she could lift my mood over the phone. "Hey, have you talked to Jake Vega lately?" I asked, noticing how many buds were beginning to peep out from the trees above us—a sure sign that spring would be in full gear soon.

Her eyebrows knit together in thought. "No, can't say that I have. He doesn't do much around town except hand out parking tickets downtown and check for fishing licenses along the canal. Why?"

Shrugging my shoulders, I just said, "I don't know. I've had three conversations with him since you left me at Prescott's yesterday morning, and I haven't talked to the kid since eighth grade."

"Didn't he move away in high school?" Sadie asked, opening the rusted iron gate at the front of the cemetery that spilled onto a dirt street behind Sheridan Avenue. The squeak it produced made me cringe momentarily as Sadie shut it.

"No. He went to high school with us," I corrected her.

Wiping the rust from the gate off her hands and onto her jeans, her face lit up with realization. "Oh! I remember. He ended up wearing dark clothes, grew his hair really long and hung out in the shadows. Completely different than the Jake from when we were in grade school." Sadie paused and turned to poke me with her finger. "In fact, you used to have a crush on him."

Before I could open my mouth and deny it, Sadie held up a hand and remarked, "Yes you did. Our freshman year. Before he went all dark-lord. The entire month of October, you would take the longest route to the cafeteria because you knew he was in Mr. Glouster's English class during our lunch and you'd hope he'd bump into you on his way inside."

My face grew warm. "Geez, Sadie. It scares me the things you remember."

A smug smile crept over her lips until she added, "And yet the same girl always ends up losing her cell phone." Sadie then padded down her pockets until she found her cell phone in the back pocket of her gray jeans and checked it for messages.

I rolled my eyes as we walked between the hardware store and the inn. "What did you need to get again?" I asked Sadie as we crossed Main Street. Sadie was a nurse in the pediatric ward of the fancy new hospital on the west side of town. Once a month, the off-duty nurses would do an activity with the kids and Sadie planned on creating a trail mix activity that involved a children's book on math.

Sadie pocketed her cell phone and pulled out a folded piece of yellow notebook paper from her front pocket. "Pretzels, chocolate candies, marshmallows, raisins, and plastic baggies."

Lacking the enthusiasm to hunt down those items, my mind fluttered back to my life in Albuquerque. When Sadie had talked about doing this activity with the children, I'd felt a stab of guilt for leaving my ELL classroom before the end of the year and wondered how they were doing. Many of the students were refugees or immigrants who just wanted to be loved, to have a stable environment, and I'd let them down. I'd had old co-workers reach out to me via social media and email, but I hadn't the heart to respond to them just yet. "I'll meet you at check out, Sadie. I think I need a cupcake," I admitted as we walked through the glass door. A little gooey mound of chocolate and sugar would only be a temporary cure for my guilt, but I didn't care.

As I walked through the aisles of people toting baskets and pushing shopping carts, it was hard to believe that a murder had just taken place here only twenty-four hours ago. Children were running up and down the aisles, a man stood in the liquor aisle already with a six-pack under his arm, and pop music was drifting from the radio by the cash register. It was almost as if the store was in denial.

Shaking my head, I followed my nose to the bakery which was at the far end of the store, just beside the set of employee doors, and I was severely craving some sugar-coated relief from the guilt-ridden thoughts invading my head. The scent of freshly baked bread grew stronger, leading me to the counter. As I perused the single serving, extra large, red velvet cupcakes made from the infamous Aunt Muriel's Sugar Shop Kitchen—a local delicacy—I heard a loud metal slamming emerge from behind the door marked Employees Only.

I looked up but no one was around to confirm my concern, so I shrugged it off as a butterfingered employee in the stock room. As I lowered my head again to the collection of cupcakes, loud voices began to travel down the hallway that gave me a bad feeling. Since no one was around, I found it hard to ignore. If someone was in trouble, I didn't want to be responsible for them not getting the help they needed. When the muffled yelling didn't stop, my nosy Alton blood kicked in and I began to travel past the door under the ruse of helping calm a squabble.

"I can't believe you!" a young woman's voice was yelling. It sounded like she'd plopped something down on a table.

"Please, keep your voice down. I can explain everything!" I recognized that voice immediately. It was Jim Browski's, the store manager. At the end of the hall, I could see that his office door was half open and another shadow was pacing wildly on the wall.

"She was seventeen years old! How dare you!" A woman came into view momentarily as she paced by the door, holding what looked like a slew of notebook paper in her hand. She looked just like the Sara I'd met two nights ago, except her hair was long and brown, and she was taller, her body and clothing more mature.

"I know. It was a mistake," Jim pleaded.

"A mistake? A mistake?!" she shrieked, moving back toward the desk. I watched as her shadow read from the papers in her hand. "'I loved the way those jeans hugged your ass.'" She shuffled to another page. "'I was going to come into your office and ask for a raise—just like the one you gave me Tuesday night.'"

Her shadow leaned over the desk. "Tell me right here, right now," she demanded, pounding the desk with her fist as she talked, "what exactly happened between you and my sister!"

The loading dock doors were open and I stood in the entrance ready to jump into the office if needed (or to run outside in order to avoid getting caught eavesdropping!). "Nothing, I swear! Just a few harmless letters were exchanged. Nothing came from them. I swear. On my child's life, I swear it," Jim exclaimed. His shadow caught his heavy head in his hands.

"What else will I find in her work locker?" the woman asked. "The murder weapon? Blackmail? A sex tape? What ever happened between you and my sister, I *will* get to the bottom of it. You can mark my words!"

As her footsteps got louder, I saw Jim's shadow grab her by the arm. "Please!" he begged. "I have a wife and a son."

"Then maybe I should take this to the police; they'd be better off without you," she said in vile disgust, and pried Jim's hand from her arm.

I ducked outside the loading dock doors just as she darted into the hallway. Peeking back inside, I saw Jim's silhouette in the door frame as he sighed heavily and ran a hand through his cotton-candy hair.

For several minutes, I stood in the alley urging my heart to steady its beating while biting my lip and trying to decide what to do. In the end, I took out my cell phone and fished out Jake's card from my sweater pocket and dialed the number.

"Deputy Jake Vega," he answered.

"Hi, Jake; it's Charli," I said, trying not to trail off. I kicked a cigarette butt off the cement ramp and leaned against the rusted iron railings, facing the back of Sadie's house.

"Hey, Charli, what can I do for you?" his voice was upbeat and I could hear the shuffling of papers and voices in the background. He was undoubtedly at the police station.

Removing myself from the loading dock, I began to walk down the alley and into the parking lot in order to loop to the front of the store as I talked. "Something weird just happened at Prescott's," I began, but found it difficult to continue.

"Did the Pineapple Bowl begin? Is there a mad dash for the sale on jam?" Jake joked.

As I reached the sidewalk on Main, I walked past people I barely knew, but felt like I had to protect them. "No, Jake. I don't want to be dramatic, but I think it deals with Sara's case." As I watched a mother exit Prescott's with a toddler who ran to his plastic tricycle parked out front, I proceeded to tell him about the turn of events that I'd witnessed from my hiding place.

When I finished, I winced, hoping he wouldn't scold me for wasting his time. He let out a deep breath and said, matter-of-factly, "I'll be right there," and hung up the phone.

CHAPTER 10

Sadie found me parked on the tri-town bus stop bench in front of Prescott's just as Jake pulled up in his ancient station wagon. The Alton Oaks Police Department decal on the side door was drastically more modern than the rest of the car which showed years of weather-wear, dents, scratches, and corners of rust. "I can't believe that old thing still works," Sadie said, plopping down beside me as Jake walked onto the curb.

Jake nodded, touching the wide brim of his deputy hat in greeting. "I keep telling the chief we should invest in more bicycles, but his heart beats in the past." He stood in front of Sadie and me in his unwrinkled uniform and pulled out his Steno pad. "So, tell me again exactly what happened."

Sadie glanced at me confused. I looked from her to Jake and explained. Going into as much detail as I could remember, I repeated everything that had happened while Sadie gaped at me with an open mouth in disbelief. "And when did this happen, approximately?" Jake asked, with one foot on the curb and the other on the street.

Squinting, I looked up at him and replied, "About fifteen minutes ago, give or take."

After glancing at his wristwatch and writing the last of his notes, Jake scratched his chin and finally said, "Thanks for the tip, Charli. The department will investigate it further. Please let me know if you hear of anything else."

Smiling in response to his no-nonsense, duty-driven

spiel, I watched Jake touch the brim of his hat once again in departure, and he walked past us through the glass doors of Prescott's Grocery.

"*Girl*," Sadie started with fierceness, "next time we come here, I'm sticking by your side. You get all the juicy details."

"Trust me," I said, "I'm not looking to get into the middle of anything, especially not this murder case."

Sadie threw me an incredulous look. "Sorry," she said sarcastically. "Totally thought you were my friend Charli, the daughter of an Alton."

I dramatically rolled my eyes at her because she was right. "Fine; I eavesdropped, but I can't help it."

"Ah, there she is. There's my Charli, my nosy little Alton," she taunted, poking me in the ribs with her elbow.

I sighed, giving into my heritage.

"Hey, remember that time in junior high when we snuck out to the creek in the woods in the middle of the night?" Sadie asked, her gaze lost in a memory.

I shook my head. We snuck out a lot, but not to drink or have sex. We did stupid stuff like poke the dead coyote who'd already been picked at by scavengers with a stick, or read ghost stories in the woods where we couldn't see the lights of our houses or hear the cars on the highway. Once we even took fishing line and tied it to several tree branches so they were bent in an unnatural way and lured Jake there the next evening after a spooky story about the Old Oak Witch. I don't think he ever went back into the woods with us again.

Sadie rested her elbow on the back of the bench and rested her head on her knuckles, studying a memory as a breeze shifted her locks. "We were having a sleepover at your house and we were sitting on your porch swing, in the dark. You turned the porch light off because of all the bugs. And we saw two people come down Oak and cross your yard. Don't you remember?" Sadie asked, her eyes moving to my face.

Again I shook my head.

"We were in eighth grade, I think. You put a hand in front of my mouth so you could hear what they were talking about, but couldn't hear 'cause they were too far away. When they disappeared behind your house, you got up and ninja'ed your way across the porch and into the bushes. I don't even think you knew what you were doing or that you left me. I followed you, following them all the way to our boundary line. I told you that we had to go back, but you insisted that two people out this late, so far secluded from town, must be up to something and it was worth the risk. You marched right past our boundary without so much as a second thought. That's when I fully understood what it was like to have Alton blood. That fearless determination for the truth— it's not always gossip, you know," Sadie said, running her fingers through her straight auburn hair absent-mindedly.

"I have no memory of this," I admitted. "What happened? Who were they?"

Sadie laughed. "I rest my case."

"No, really," I urged, turning to face her fully. "This is going to bother me. Fill in the blanks."

Still smiling, Sadie shook her head and said, "It was your brother..." she trailed off looking for a sign of recognition in my face.

"With a girl..." she added, hoping I'd catch on.

Sadie's smile didn't diminish as she continued, "When we caught up to them at the creek, they were—"

"Oh!" I remembered and my face grew red and I raised both hands to cover it. "Dammit, Sadie! I buried that memory for a reason. Why did you have to go and dig it up?"

Sadie only laughed, finding my reaction priceless. Her phone vibrated and, still laughing, she reached for it in her back pocket. Now frowning, she looked from her phone to me and said, "Oh, good gravy, I need to get going, Charli. I'm doing a double shift. I'll call you when I'm sane again." Before she got up from the spot on the bench, she turned to me with a stern finger in my face and added, "Don't get into too much trouble, young lady!"

I lifted my hands defensively and she laughed. "Be safe," she said with a quick hug. "Geez, I never thought I'd have to say that in Alton Oaks," she mused as she got up and stretched. The plastic Prescott's bag that carried her supplies crinkled as she moved.

Smiling, I replied, "I hope your activity goes well, Sadie." She gave me a genuine smile and endearingly touched the top of my head in reply. Then, as fast as her little legs could carry her, she dashed across the parking lot and up the stairs to her apartment.

I had nothing else planned for the day so I thought I'd take my time walking home; maybe I'd take my camera out on a stroll and take Jake's advice with the town newspaper, *The Oak Leaf Press*.

Deep in my thoughts and daydreams, I didn't hear him approach me as I passed the junior high school. "Hey!" The word pierced through the air like an arrow. His dark figure was emerging from the man-made path between the back of the school and the Kratsky's house.

Rip Oakley was walking up to me in his tough-guy swagger and I froze with alarm, like a child getting caught with their hand in the cookie jar. Lord help me if I was ever in a fight-or-flight situation.

He wore dark jeans with a black shirt under his black leather jacket—which was uncalled for—it was a beautiful day. Maybe it was his version of body armor.

Rip came face-to-face with me and his whole

presence was dark and foreboding. It was a knock-em-down-while-they're-still-standing attitude that dripped with self-righteous disdain. It was scary, but in a heart-fluttering, bad boy kind of way that I hated myself for feeling.

"You," he said with a Chicago accent, singling me out as if there were others around. Then it hit me with sobering realization that *no one else was around.* School was still in session and the Alton House was way out there in the distance. Not a soul would cross this path until three o'clock when the junior high kids would congregate nearby off school property or rush to the Canal Trail to hang out. Hopefully, they didn't come across my lifeless body when they did.

He looked down at me with his hard amber eyes, accusingly. This guy must have majored in school bullying and minored in intimidation at the school of Hard Knocks. "Hear you've been talking to the police about me."

With my guard up, I tried not to act so intimidated. "Not intentionally," I offered.

"You got a problem with me in this town?" When he talked, I noticed that his feet were firmly planted shoulder-width apart and his knees were slightly bent. It was probably from years of expecting a punch when he talked. I didn't blame him. And the finger on his right hand came dangerously close to poking me in the shoulder with his accusations, but he seemed to control his temper enough not to touch me.

He ended his question using my full name, undoubtedly a tactic of intimidation. "Charli," he spit the words from his mouth, "Parker."

Man, this guy was giving me a mad case of the goose bumps and it took a lot of effort to not let a wave of shivers shake my body. I studied him, desperately trying to keep emotion from my face.

"Well, do ya?" he asked when I didn't answer. "You got a problem with me in your town, Charli Parker? Because I'll tell you what: I don't appreciate being questioned by police the second I get into town."

He was being awfully offensive for my understandable mistake. "Look," I said, finding my courage, taking on a dauntless tone. "It was a mistake. It's a small town. Everybody knows everything and everyone. And you were walking into a house that's been vacant since before I was born and no one knew who you were." I was on a roll now. The anger I'd been pushing down about my broken marriage was starting to seep out and this poor guy was about to get a taste of it. "I'm sorry you took offense to our neighborhood watch," I said with growing agitation, my words slathered in attitude and misplaced emotion. "It's not like I called up the police and said, 'Oh, a scary man is on the loose!' Buck up, buddy," I said, poking his jacket; the gesture surprised me, but I didn't let it show. "Welcome to small town living."

I dared to take a step closer to him and he let surprise flicker in his gold-flecked eyes for a moment. In an unnerving, deeper voice that scared even me, I added, "I don't know if you've heard, but a dead girl turned up at *our* grocery store. The whole town is a little on edge." I took a step back and started to walk away. Before I walked past him, I added, "So welcome to the neighborhood, neighbor."

With that, I turned on my heel and walked hastily up the street, letting my hands shake and lips quiver with adrenaline the entire way back to the Alton house.

CHAPTER 11

When I walked in the front door, the plastic canvas hanging at the living room's entrance to my left whooshed with the draft my movement had made. "You hungry, Charli?" My mother's voice traveled from the kitchen with the scent of spices—tacos!

"Yes!" I said, my stomach grumbling at the scent as I made my way down the short hallway.

My mother was putting a bowl of salad greens on the kitchen table; she must have just gotten home from the library since her black framed cat-eye style glasses were still resting on the top of her head. Eighties music drifted from the radio on the windowsill with the sunshine. My mother looked up at me and smiled at my enthusiasm. "Good. I made enough for two."

Sitting down at the table, I eagerly grabbed a dish. Mom filled her plate and watched me out of the corner of her eyes build a taco of ground beef, salad greens, cheese, green onion, cilantro, and sour cream. After taking a large bite, Mom asked, "So how do you like it?"

"It's different," I admitted with a full mouth. "Is this ground turkey?" I asked, swallowing.

Mom took her time chewing the bite in her mouth. "Do you like it?" she asked.

I squeezed the juice of half a lime onto my taco and slowly ate another bite. I shrugged in response to her question. "It's okay." As I rolled the textures around in my mouth, I suddenly realized why my mother was avoiding my question. "Mom," I started, putting down my taco. "What exactly am I eating?"

Mom shifted in her seat before answering. "Nothing bad. You liked it, remember."

"I said it was okay," I corrected, wiping my hands on a napkin.

"Well, it's not ground beef; it's walnuts. And the sour cream is made from cashews. And I made the cheese from almond milk. Do you like it?" Her face was so full of hope, I didn't have the heart to put down her taste in food. I nodded hesitantly and decided to take at least one more bite.

Mom beamed as she happily munched on her dinner. "So how long are you planning on staying with us?" she asked after taking a sip from her half gallon jug of water that she carried with her everywhere.

"Is this my eviction notice?" I asked, raising my eyebrow and absentmindedly taking another bite of my taco.

"No," she said, wiping her mouth with a napkin from the rooster-themed napkin holder my grandmother had made in the seventies. "I'm just wondering what your plans are."

Pushing the plate that carried the entrails of my taco away, I sighed. "I don't know, Mom. I've only been home for two days. Can we talk about this later? Can I have a week to sort out my thoughts?" I realized my tone had become defensive and my features were hard, so I kept my head down and stared at the crumbs where my plate had been.

The sound of an electric guitar solo played over the radio and my mother pushed out her chair, the wooden legs scraping against the floor. "Take all the time you need, Charli." Her voice was soft and full of acceptance. "I like having you back home."

My features softened and I was relieved she didn't push the matter or dig for some more information.

Maybe this new healthy lifestyle of hers was affecting her empathy... or maybe this was just a side of my mother I'd never experienced before. "Thanks, Mom," I said.

She stood up and poured herself a mug of tea from the kettle that had been cooling on the stove. The sun was beginning to set and the world outside the kitchen window was bright with the glow of the dying sun. "Why don't you come sit on the porch with me for a while?" she asked, fiddling with the handle on her Branson, Missouri, souvenir mug. "I promise we won't talk about anything Albuquerque related. We don't have to talk at all. We can just watch the sunset like we used to do when you were little."

When Bailey was still a baby, Mom would bring me outside and brush my hair before bedtime. In the summer, if Bailey was still sleeping, I would also get to curl up on the porch swing with Mom and read a story. The nostalgia grabbed a hold of me like a bear hug so I nodded.

Following my mother onto the porch, I grabbed a flannel blanket that was draped over the bannister before walking out the door. We sat on the porch swing, sharing the warmth of the blanket, and relaxing in the rhythm of the swing. In comfortable silence, we watched how the sun hit the trees to the south, dancing off the buds and premature leaves that had survived last night's windstorm. Winter had officially left western Illinois and soon we would be sweating in the humidity and swatting away the mosquitos.

When the sky turned a dusty blue-gray with a faint glow on the western horizon, the headlights of Mrs. Kratsky's golf cart came into view. She honked her *hee-haw, hee-haw* horn as she pulled up into the driveway, and both Jenna and Bailey's porch lights flickered on only minutes after.

As the stars started piercing through the sky, Bailey, Mrs. Kratsky and Jenna all sat down with their after-dinner coffees, fully intent on trading gossip—their niceties down to a bare minimum. After Mrs. Kratsky shared about the great deal she'd gotten on pork chops in Terryville, the conversation took the turn they were all waiting for.

"Speaking of groceries," Bailey started, crossing her legs from her spot on the wooden bench, "I heard a rumor that someone here overheard a conversation at Prescott's today that led to a police visit."

Everyone looked around and denied it was them. A pundit grin spread across Bailey's lips as she cleared her throat and lightly kicked me with her free leg.

"Charli!" my mom exclaimed. "What happened? Why didn't you tell me the minute you came home?"

I could feel the blood rushing to my face. My sister wasn't being mean, understand. She was trying to include me in the conversation—doing a good thing to give me the attention. It was probably why we never really got along as sisters; we just didn't understand each other. "Go on, Charli," Bailey encouraged.

"I don't know," I said defensively. "I just overheard a conversation between Jim and a woman."

Bailey couldn't keep it in anymore. She leaned forward and the words spilled from her mouth. I was grateful that everyone's heads turned in her direction. "Deanna McCormick was at the deli in Prescott's this afternoon. The butcher—what's his name?"

"Frank," Jenna offered, her short blonde hair moving like drapes in the breeze of an open window.

"Yeah, Frank was behind the counter talking to Jim, and then Jake Vega comes in and asks to speak with Jim. And you know Deanna, she eavesdropped as much as she could, but all she got was 'Charli,' 'Sara,' something about letters and 'Sandy' who's Sara's sister," Bailey explained.

"So what happened?" Jenna asked, urging me for information.

Is this who I was now? One of my mom's gossip girls? At least they weren't hammering me for details about my marriage, I guess. Groaning, I gave in. "Sandy found letters that put Jim in a bad light. I don't know what they said, but it sounds like Sandy found them in Sara's employee locker."

"And how did you hear this? Where were you?" Bailey asked, leaning forward. The bench beneath her groaned as her weight shifted.

I felt my face grow warm again and I focused on the dead leaves that winter had forgotten to swallow as they scraped across the porch in the breeze. "I was at the bakery," I shared. "I was shopping for a cupcake and I overheard them yelling at each other in his office." I frowned slightly when I realized that I never did get that cupcake.

"I knew it was Jim!" Jenna declared, slapping her thigh. "He was always a bit creepy."

"No, it's not Jim. It's probably Sandy—it's always the one you least suspect," Mrs. Kratsky chimed in, giving an all-knowing nod. The brown plastic headband that tamed her shoulder-length gray hair shifted with the gesture.

Mom only took in everyone's information, not leaning one way or the other, and sipped her coffee beside me.

"What about the stranger who moved in across the street?" Bailey asked. "It's all I heard about at the pre-school Moms' meeting." Bailey's gaze drifted towards the no-longer empty house and added a bit dreamily, "I hear he's a hell of a man."

Mrs. Kratsky chimed in right away. "Oh, he's new in town. Straight outta Chicago. He was a journalist, or undercover cop, or something. I'm not sure. Heard he inherited the house, but others say he bought it. Someone even said he walked in and claimed it without money or papers and nobody wanted to confront him so they let him take the house."

I let a not-so-discreet laugh escape my mouth at Mrs. Kratsky's comment. Suddenly, I had four pairs of eyes on me and I apologized. "I'm sorry, but have you met our straight-laced deputy?" I asked, and then became interested in the dusty layer of dirt that covered the floorboards of the porch. "I doubt that happened," I added, more so under my breath than to the group.

Mrs. Kratsky only shrugged and drank from her nearly empty travel mug. "It's what I hear," she said in defense and then went on, "Well, that's not all the news in town. Seems as though a detail was slipped about Sara's case. It definitely wasn't an accident. It was murder." Gasps echoed around the circle of women in response. Even I looked up, interested in the details. "Apparently, she was stabbed with some type of knife they think. Still can't find the murder weapon." Another wave of gasps were heard around the porch as Mrs. Kratsky finished, a sign that no one had heard this juicy tidbit until now.

"They haven't found the murder weapon?" Bailey asked. She was playing with the heart-shaped pendant on her necklace, a trait she inherited from our mother.

Mrs. Kratsky shook her head and leaned back in the wooden rocking chair. Tufts of her hair got caught on the splintering wood which made her look slightly neurotic.

"That's good though, right?" Jenna asked. My mom leaned forward and I felt heat radiate off her body. I pulled the flannel blanket closer towards me to capture and save it. "I mean, the murderer must still have it, right?" Jenna continued. "We find the murder weapon, we find the murderer?"

"She has a point," my mother said, kicking the blanket off her left leg and scratching her ankle. "But who in Alton Oaks is capable of murder?"

Silence settled over the porch as we let the question sink in: who, in our small wholesome (albeit gossipy) town, was capable of murder? And not just any murder. If the rumors were true, then it was a blood-drenched, ruthless stabbing. Would we have had conversations with them? Walked by them on the street? Shared a coffee or a hello with them without knowing what they were capable of?

Jenna was the one to finally break the silence. "When was there ever a murder in Alton Oaks?" she asked, her gaze bouncing between my mother and Mrs. Kratsky.

Mom shrugged, still silently soaking in the gossip or possibly thinking about suspects.

"Never," Mrs. Kratsky said, "unless you count that car accident in the forties, but that wasn't really a murder." Her tone lowered when she added, "Or if you count Andrew Alton's." She looked towards my mother as if she'd just spilled a sacred secret, but my mother only considered the detail with the tilt of her head and took another sip of her tea.

It was true. My great-great-grandfather had been murdered on the steps of the town hall when he was thirty-eight years old and it had gone unsolved all these years. Perhaps Sara's murder was Alton Oaks' first murder in over ninety years.

There were a few moments of silence while the details settled in our minds. "Who do you think did it?" Bailey asked to no one in particular.

"Calvin was cleared; he has an alibi and witnesses," Jenna said, defensively. He was her godson, after all.

"Well, there's Jim," my mother offered, finally

speaking up. "Things aren't going well for him at all. He was apparently on a camping trip, alone, the night Sara died."

"Hmm, so no alibi, interesting," Jenna added.

"And if the letters found in Sara's locker are true, there's motive," Mrs. Kratsky pointed out.

"*And* he's creepy," Bailey added.

"And what about that new guy?" Jenna offered, nodding towards the dark house down the street. "He's standoffish. Seems aggressive. Classic murder suspect."

Stifling a giggle at her daytime drama categorizations, I had to admit she had a point. I had seen him with Sara the night she was murdered.

"Lucky we have a deputy living down the street, then," my mom said, grinning.

"Speaking of the deputy down the street," hinted Bailey. "The town's abuzz with how much they see you two together." Her eyebrows lifted in my direction.

When I realized what she was insinuating, I automatically went on the defensive. "What? No!" I exclaimed. How incredulously ridiculous. "Just work-related stuff—I have to report suspicious activity. It's my civic duty." Oh boy, was I coming off too strong? Too defensive? "I am *not* seeing him. We are not '*a thing.*' He's a friend. Just a friend." I wished I could have drawn a big period at the end of my sentence to declare the topic over, but that wouldn't have stopped the Gossip Club.

Everyone on the porch tried to hide their smirks, but the growing darkness did not do a good-enough job at hiding them. "I saw you two laughing and walking home last night," Mrs. Kratsky said jeeringly.

"Honestly," I said and looked up at the wooden beams above us in frustration. "I'm still married to Jackson."

Without skipping a beat, my sister asked, "Yeah, so

what's going on there? Are you and Jackson still together? Is he coming out here?" The porch got quiet and everyone seemed to lean forward, extremely interested in my answer. I suddenly wondered if the reason I hadn't wanted to talk about this topic to anyone was because I wasn't ready to face the truth, or if it was because I didn't know the truth.

Geez, how did the conversation get here? These were clever, sly, sneaky women who lured you in like a porch light to a moth. "I—I don't..." I looked to my mother for help. I hadn't sorted through these thoughts yet. I had only left him three days ago. I'd ignored all his calls and messages since I saw him in bed with *her*. I wasn't ready to discuss that yet.

For a brief moment, I thought Mom wouldn't rescue me from this topic. I knew it was killing her not knowing the why, the how, the what. Finally, my mother looked from me to the others and said, "Oh, leave her alone."

One by one, each person leaned back, some sighing in resignation. Bailey pursed her lips together and glanced towards the gauzy drapes in her brightly lit living room windows. Mrs. Kratsky drained the coffee in her mug, opening the lid and dumping the last drops in her mouth. And Jenna leaned over with her elbows on her knees and picked at her chipping nail polish, avoiding eye contact.

Several awkward moments passed until Mrs. Kratsky took pity on the situation. "Well, that's enough for me. I'll see you spring chickens in the morning," she said, rising from the wooden rocking chair and climbing down the creaking porch steps.

When she got into her golf cart, she flipped on the fairy lights she'd decorated the interior with so that it shed light onto the worn leather steering wheel and dashboard that carried an empty travel mug. Before peeling out of the gravel driveway, she momentarily blinded us with the extremely bright headlights, that made us groan, squint, anad avert our eyes from the yard.

As our eyes adjusted once again to the evening, Bailey rose from the bench that continued to moan with her movements and asked, "Jenna, did you want to come over and borrow that dress for the fundraiser?"

"Oh, yes," Jenna exclaimed, jumping up from her spot on the metal patio chair. She kissed my mom on the head and threw me a quick hug. They left animatedly chatting about the fundraiser ball that she and her husband attended every year for children's literacy in Davenport. Jenna and Bailey had always gotten along—almost as much as Jillian and I did. As I watched them walk across the grass, their blonde hair glowing in the moon light, I had mixed feelings; at least Bailey had a sister-like figure she got along with. But what was so wrong with me that I couldn't be that person?

When the sound of crickets and the buzzing of flies became louder than any other human sound, my mother sighed and said, "Looks like it's just you and me, kid," and took a sip that drained the last of the tea from her mug.

Before I could respond, her cell phone called for attention from the pocket of her jeans. I could tell it was my father by the harp ringtone that reminded me of flashbacks on television shows. "Well, just you," my mom corrected as she kicked off the blanket that covered our laps and walked inside to answer the call. She flipped the switch in the hallway that flooded the porch with light. Anything nearby with wings was automatically attracted to the bright light above the door.

Eagerly, I grabbed the surplus of blanket and

wrapped it around my shoulders. I sunk deeper into the corner of the swing and watched how the trees popped over the ledge on the other side of the porch, like a see-saw, with each glide of the swing. I wanted to bottle that moment because it was the first time I'd felt relaxed in such a long time.

Life was different here, compared to Albuquerque. In New Mexico, I was at work or at home. I never really found time or a place to sit outside, unless Jackson wanted to spend time with me. Albuquerque was always so loud. And hot. Our apartment was right off a busy street and even when the temperature was bearable, we couldn't open the windows because of the traffic noise.

Sitting on the porch at that moment, I closed my eyes and leaned my head back, listening to the crickets and owls coming out to enjoy it. The rise and fall of the swing was relaxing. I draped my long hair over the back of the swing and the pendulum-like movement was comforting, hypnotizing. It brought me back to my childhood, calming the storm that was constantly brewing inside me.

"Busy?" Jake's voice cut through my serenity, but it was buttery sweet and welcome in my peaceful world.

I picked my head up to see him at the top of the stairs. "Not at all," I said, sitting up, letting my cold hair drape over my shoulders. "What's up?"

"On my way home and saw you out here by yourself, which is odd. There's always a group of women on your porch. Everything okay?" He took a seat opposite of me, the rocking chair which Mrs. Kratsky had vacated moments before. He was carrying an Oakies take-out bag.

"Oh fine. The world's going topsy-turvy, or haven't you heard?" I joked. If a week ago you'd told me I would be living at my parents house in Alton Oaks, where there had been a murder, I would have thought no statement could have been more wrong. I would have bet a great deal of money against it, in fact.

"Dinner?" I asked changing my train of thought. I gestured to the Oakies bag he had set on the small table beside him which housed a dead plant.

He nodded. "I've been craving an Oakie burrito since last night."

Even though I didn't know grown-up-Jake that well, he looked drained. "Everything okay?" I asked, pulling my knees up to my chin.

He grabbed a tortilla chip from the paper bag and popped it into his mouth. "Oh, yeah," he said in between chewing. He waved his hand dismissively as if the weight on his shoulders was no big deal. "This case is overwhelming our small department. I've been working eighteen hour days. On top of that, we have other officials in from out-of-town since it's a murder case and the department is chaotic. The mayor is constantly calling for updates." Jake briefly turned around towards Jenna's house where my uncle, the mayor, resided. When he realized the coast was clear, he continued, "Alton Oaks now has a murder rate, can you believe it?"

I shook my head; it was hard to believe. Normally the only bad thing that ever happened in Alton Oaks was a bicycle theft or a fender bender by some Canary downtown. "It's affecting tourism. Our town can't afford that," he added solemnly.

A few moments passed, filled only with the sounds of nocturnal animals. A cold breeze passed by which caused me to pull the blanket tighter around my shoulders. Being in Albuquerque for so long had definitely affected my tolerance for what Illinoisans defined as spring weather. It was going to be an interesting winter... if I decided to stay.

Finally, I asked, "Do you regret it? Going to the academy instead of U of I?"

He looked at me like I was crazy as he chewed through another tortilla chip. "No." He laughed and brushed the salt and grease from his hands. "I guess I didn't tell you the whole story," he said and moved the Oakies take-out bag away from him.

I didn't say anything to change the subject, so he went on. "So I left Bloomington to go to the academy and became a police officer. Afterwards, I worked on the police force in Normal while getting my degree in criminal justice. I went back to school to get my Bachelor's because I wanted to be a detective, but in the end I missed Alton Oaks too much and, as you know, our department isn't big enough to have full-time detectives on the force."

"Hmm," I mused, letting his words paint a picture in my mind. "So this case is a taste of what you could have had as a homicide detective, huh?"

He laughed. "Yeah. Kinda, sorta," he answered. Creases appeared in the corners of his eyes when he laughed and I liked that. He looked more like his dad when he laughed.

Just then his cell phone rang. "Sorry," he said, leaning over and reaching into his pocket.

He got up and stood by the stairs as he answered the phone. After several curt answers to the person on the other end, he hung up and sighed.

He came back to where I was sitting without a word. "Let me guess, you can't tell me?" I said, assuming the phone call was work related.

"We were just granted a search warrant," he divulged, closing the grease-spotted paper bag that held his tortilla chips.

"For what?" I asked.

He pursed his lips together and lifted his eyebrows,

shrugging.

I let out a dramatic sigh. "You can't tell me."

"Oh, I could," he said, playfully, and picked up the Oakies take-out bag.

"Then why won't you?" I asked, planting my feet on the ground and letting the blanket fall into my lap.

"Because the Gossip Queen is listening in from the dining room window," he said in a low tone. Then, in a much bolder voice he called out, "Bye, Mrs. Parker!" Jake waved to the window as he descended the stairs. When he reached the gravel, he put his dinner in the basket of his bicycle and put on his helmet. Before departing, he turned to me and said, "See you around, Charli."

I waved, watching him disappear into the shadows. Then I turned to the window and lifted an eyebrow at my mother. "Not seeing each other, huh?" she mocked from the other side of the screen.

I rolled my eyes and hid my chagrin as I picked up the blanket and buried myself in it.

CHAPTER 12

The next morning the sun was shining and the temperature had reached sixty-five by eight o'clock—it was going to be a good day. I pulled my bike out of the garage and half wheeled/half dragged the poor thing to Mr. Kratsky's garage for a consultation. If I was going to be in Alton Oaks for a while, I needed a faster way to get to and from town.

As I made my way down Oak, I was working up a sweat fighting with the bicycle. The wheels were in such bad shape that the tires were coming off and the rims were getting dented and damaged from the gravel road. Practically carrying the bike down the road, I was suddenly aware that I had forgotten to apply deodorant that morning and was relieved when the Kratsky's driveway came into view. The sounds of children laughing and yelling echoed off the buildings and onto the Kratsky property as they waited for school to start.

Mr. Kratsky was a short round man who always wore overalls that never really covered his ankles. He used to be a mechanic in Terryville, but loved to rebuild and fix bicycles; he made a pretty penny on the side from the Canaries who bought his bikes through his newspaper and online advertisements. When the fancy bike shops in town had old bicycles or odd parts, Mr. K. would sometimes buy them, but more often he'd salvage them from the dump. It didn't hurt that his garage was adjacent to the schools and the man-made path to the Canal Trail. The kids in town would always stop by after school for Mr. K (how we all affectionately addressed him) to fix a flat tire or a broken chain. At three o'clock, when the dismissal bell rang, he was always ready in his driveway with an air pump close by.

When I reached his driveway, he was removing a wheel from a child's frilly pink bicycle that sat upside down on his work bench. As the sound of the dragging tires and my huffing and puffing got closer, he looked over his shoulder and smiled.

"Charli!" he greeted me with arms wide open, waddling towards me with a screwdriver in his hand and chain oil smeared on his cheek. "Welcome home!" His hugs always smelled of motor oil and turpentine.

"Thanks, Mr. K.," I said, hoping I didn't smell from my unexpected morning workout. "How's business?" I asked, placing my hands back onto the handlebars of my bike. He motioned for me to follow him to his garage where a record player was playing a scratchy rendition of Elvis' "Jailhouse Rock."

"Oh, never better. Just picked up a handful of old Schwinns from a garage sale in Morris that I'm refurbishing. Eight bicycles for five bucks! Can you believe it?"

I smiled at his enthusiasm. "You sure have a different definition of retirement than most people I know."

"Oh, Charli, Retirement's about having fun and doing what you love and I've nailed it on the head." He was always so animated when he talked and used his hands to imitate hammering a nail to make his point.

"Well, then, I've brought you a challenge," I said, motioning to my bike.

Mr. Kratsky dramatically grabbed his chest and gasped, kneeling to stroke the bike. "Oh my dear. What did the mean old Charli do to you?" He jokingly gave me a dirty look. "You used to love this bike." He stood up and took the bike's handlebars, gently guiding it the rest of the way to his workshop.

"I remember the day you got this bike," he mused. "Your dad gave it to you for your twelfth birthday. You named it Prince Ezra and would have me give it a check up every other day." He parked it at the entrance of his garage and pulled out a rag from his back pocket.

"Well, I'm not getting rid of it," I said defensively, remembering the adventures we'd had: races down Black Hill Avenue, trips to Froz T's, family rides down the Canal Bike Path, and, best of all, I could stay out later because, with a bicycle, I could get home faster before my curfew. "I love it too much, which is why I left it here instead of taking it with me to New Mexico. I was wondering if you could fix it up—*can* it be saved?"

"Oh, Charli," he said with a concerned look, "didn't you hear? I can fix anything on wheels." He laughed and looked the bike over once more, fiddling with different parts. "It's not in that bad of a condition. I can get it back to you in a week—maybe two—and you'll never recognize it."

"Thanks, Mr. K.," I said relieved. "I knew I could count on you." I gave him another hug before leaving his backyard.

As I walked down his driveway and to the front of the house, the school bell had rung and the kids were filing into the school. Parents began departing down the streets on their bicycles and pushing their strollers. "Oh, Charli!"

I turned to see Jim Browski's wife, Tammy, approaching the driveway with a child on a plastic tricycle. I didn't really know her, but I remember riding the bus with her to school. She was one of the few seniors who rode the bus when I was a freshman. "Oh, hi, Tammy," I said, backtracking.

"You've moved back then? It's true?" she asked, moving her feet to be sure they weren't run over by the tricycle.

I shrugged and mentally prepared myself for another one of these conversations. "For the time being, yeah."

"You were teaching in Texas, right?" The little boy rode his tricycle in a few tight circles around us before pedaling it up and down the Kratsky's driveway.

"New Mexico, actually," I said, brushing my bangs out of my eyes. I made a mental note to get them trimmed as soon as possible. "I was teaching English Language Learners."

"Oh, good," she said, not really registering my words. "Listen, I have some old teaching supplies sitting in the garage. Would you want to take a look? I don't think I'll be teaching anytime soon." She rested a hand on her stomach and even in her bulky sweater, I could see her stomach swelled with a healthy child.

"Yeah, that'd be great," I said. Even though I didn't have a classroom right then, free teaching supplies are free teaching supplies. I wasn't going to say no, especially since I'd left everything I had in New Mexico.

"Great!" she said and checked her wristwatch. "How's noon?" she asked, bending down and grabbing the handlebars of the tricycle to stop her son from making another round up the driveway.

The boy started making fussy noises and I wanted to leave the scene before it erupted into a full tantrum. "Excellent. I'll see you then," I said, turning to head home, hoping it was the end of the conversation.

Tammy had directed the boy in the tricycle to the north and she chased him as he took off and crossed Oak Street.

Minutes later, as I walked past my cousin Jillian's

house, with her wind chimes and bird feeders swaying in the distant breeze, I noticed the sheriff's station wagon parked in front of Rip's darkened, weather-beaten house a few acres ahead of me.

As I walked past the house, nothing transpired, not even the whisper of a conversation. Continuing on my path, I looked over my shoulder every so often, hoping to catch a clue as to what was happening. Slowly, I walked up the creaking stairs to the Alton house, even stopping to tie my shoes. Lingering by the front door, I strained my eyes to focus on the front porch several acres away. About to give up, I placed my hand on the doorknob to walk inside, but decided to throw one last glance toward that old house.

When I saw movement, I left the door and leaned over the porch ledge like a nosy Alton. Jake and Sheriff Gomes had exited the house and were escorting Rip to the station wagon. I watched as Rip sat in the backseat, Jake went in the passenger door, and Sheriff Gomes took his time squeezing into the driver's seat. After they drove away and the dust from the road plumed into the air, I jumped through the front door. "Mom!" I yelled into the house. She would know what was happening.

CHAPTER 13

When I found my mother, she had just gotten out of the shower. "Mom?" I asked, swinging into her room with my hands on the oak doorframe. Layers of varnish had chipped off over the years and with my touch, a bit more crumbled into my hands.

She sat on the edge of her bed in a bathrobe and her hair wrapped in a baby blue towel. She was rubbing lotion on her hands and looked alarmed when I entered the room short of breath. Before she could ask what had happened, I blurted out, "Mom! I was just walking home and Sheriff Gomes and Jake were escorting Rip out of his house. Left in the station wagon. What happened?"

My mother looked from me to her bedroom window, which was open and the light breeze danced with the curtain. Words seemed to escape her. She walked towards the door, then turned to grab her cell phone from the dresser. She backtracked to her closet. "Give me a few minutes, Charli," she said a bit harried. I backed out of the bedroom, wondering if she knew anything at all.

Within minutes, I heard the slamming of the screen door and rushed to the window to see who it was. My mother had thrown on an outfit and walked out the door, throwing the baby blue towel off her head as she sprinted down the driveway towards her bicycle, cell phone to her ear.

Left behind, my curiosity deflated slightly. As I watched my mother leave a trail of dust behind her from the window of my bedroom, I fell onto my unmade bed. *I guess I'll find out one way or another,* I thought and sighed, wondering what was happening to me—my curious Alton blood was pumping in full force.

My camera bag sat beneath my bedside table so I decided to distract myself. After all, I had no plans until noon and I didn't want to work on my personal issues just yet. So I slung the strap over my shoulder and made my way to the front porch, grabbing a glass of iced tea on the way.

The day had warmed up considerably already and I was almost feeling too warm in my sweater. I slipped off my shoes, pulled my camera out, and leaned back into the swing. Listening to a bird chirping in a tree nearby, I flipped through pictures of the street art and murals of Albuquerque's cityscape and the pictures of the desert from a long ago road trip with Jackson. It had been a long time since I'd used my camera.

As I flipped through the pictures on my memory card, I sighed and debated whether or not to delete them. My hand unconsciously found its way to my cell phone and I stared at the envelope icon, knowing I had unread messages and voicemails from Jackson. What was I waiting for? Nothing.

Honestly, I was afraid.

Was I afraid I'd go back to him? Was I afraid I was wrong? A failure? Was I afraid of his reaction? I bit my lip and studied the picture of us when we'd returned from serving with the Peace Corps in Costa Rica. During my second year of service, I'd started teaching English as a Foreign Language and had met Jackson. His dirty blonde hair was in dreadlocks and he was always smiling. I think it was his smile that I fell in love with. It radiated joy and warmth. His term of service ended a few months before mine did, but he stayed in Costa Rica. He had bought an old van that he lived out of and he stayed because of me.

When my term ended, we decided to drive up from Latin America and through Mexico together. His family was from Santa Fe and he always dreamed of opening an art studio in Albuquerque. The picture had been taken at a local cafe as soon as we arrived in Albuquerque. We were tan, windswept, greasy, and dirty in the photo, but we were so happy. He wore an old brown t-shirt with a pair of frayed jean shorts that had once been pants. I wore a tie-dyed shirt from when I was a volunteer lifeguard at the YMCA in college. The way Jackson's arm wrapped around my shoulders in the picture and the way my eyes creased when I smiled showed how jubilant we were. A warm tear fell down my cheek and I had to look away from memories I didn't want to face.

Down Oak, I saw a cloud of dust without the bulk of a vehicle in front of it. Checking the time, I realized that it was nearly eleven o'clock and I could just make out my mother pedaling up the road.

I shut down my camera and stowed it in its case. Then I wiped my eyes and tried to shift back into my Alton Oaks personality before my mother pulled into the driveway. Hopefully, she'd be too distracted by gossip to notice the redness around my glassy eyes.

As she put her kick-stand in place, I walked to the porch stairs. "Well?" I asked.

Mom pulled a water bottle out of her fanny pack, relishing the moment. After a few chugs, she walked to where I was, recapping the bottle. Her face was glistening and dirt from the road stuck to the beads of sweat on her temples. She sat on the top stair, wiping her temples with the back of her long-sleeve shirt. "Jake's search warrant was for Jim's office and Sara's employee locker. They found a cigarette lighter in

Sara's locker with Rip Oakley's fingerprints on it," she finally shared.

"Wow," I said and remembered how Rip's presence was both exciting and terrifying. A small wave of goose bumps rippled down my back.

"Apparently, Rip has a record for assault, so..." Mom took another swig of water, catching her breath. "That's all I could find out, but there's gotta be more to the story. I'm going to grab a quick lunch and walk down to Mrs. Kratsky's. Wanna tag along?" she asked, nudging me with her elbow; she was clearly on an endorphin high, but I wasn't sure if it was from the exercise or the hunt for fresh gossip.

Feigning disappointment, I replied, "I can't. I'm supposed to meet Tammy Browski for some teaching supplies."

"Teaching supplies? Did you get an offer to teach?" my mother asked optimistically.

I shook my head. "No, but in case I do, I'll be ready." I didn't have the heart to tell her that I wasn't actively looking to teach since I only had ELL and TEFL licenses, not a general education one.

She tapped my knee with her hand reassuringly. "Don't worry. Something will come along," she said and stood up, stretching. "Want me to call you if I find anything out?"

"Um, sure," I said hesitantly, realizing how much of my Alton was showing with my need for information.

Mom threw me a double thumbs up and jogged up the stairs, letting the screen door slam shut behind her.

Tammy and Jim lived on Second Street East, which was close to downtown. I decided to use Mom's bike since it was still parked in the driveway and had plenty of basket space to store any teaching supplies I might want to take.

As I rode down Oak, I passed Mrs. Kratsky on her golf cart and she pulled over after she noticed I had slowed to a stop. "What's shakin'?" she asked, her hands planted on the steering wheel and Diana Ross belting out a tune from the portable radio that was secured to the dashboard with a bungee cord. "Mom's looking for you," I said, giving her a heads up.

She rubbed her hands together in anticipation. "Oh good. Cause I have news for her." She then drove off toward the Alton House without saying goodbye, and I only laughed: small town entertainment.

After pulling into Tammy's driveway, I noticed a paper plate taped to the front door that read, "Go to back door," in blue crayon. After parking my bike in the paved driveway (what luxury these close-to-town people have), I knocked on the screen door. The storm door was open and I could hear the sound of a child singing and banging on something, while the smell of chicken nuggets and ketchup traveled past the screen in front of me.

"Oh, hi, Charli!" Tammy greeted me as she walked towards the door. Her son was at her ankles, nearly making her trip. She picked him up and rested him on her hip—her belly bigger than ever—just as she reached me. Coming outside, she said, "I'm glad you came. It's all in the garage." She motioned for me to follow her down the small cemented path. Tammy placed the child in the sandbox just beside the building and added, "I hope you can use most of it—I won't be offended if you can't. Here, help me with this door."

When Tammy and I lifted the garage door, the sun sent the shadows retreating back into their corners like cockroaches and shed light upon years of clutter, dust, and what I hoped were cobwebs. The garage was small; it could barely have fit one car, not that it did. Old dressers, a broken sewing machine, sports equipment, unmarked boxes, bicycles, holiday decorations, and outdoor gear were stacked in an unorganized fashion.

The dust danced in the sunlight as Tammy put her hands on her hips. "The shelf in that corner has all my teaching supplies," she said, pointing to the far side of the garage. "You help yourself; I'm afraid I can't be of any help," she said, gesturing towards her stomach. "I'd do nothing but knock things down—I might get buried alive."

I half-heartedly laughed and said, "Oh, I understand. Thank you for thinking of me; I hope I can use this stuff."

Tammy smiled and rubbed her stomach like most pregnant women do. "You're lucky you were the first teacher I saw. Anyway, you help yourself and take your time. I'm gonna see if James is ready for his nap." She turned to go, but then stopped and added, "If you hear blood-curdling cries from the house, it's just my headstrong child refusing to sleep."

I smiled and watched Tammy waddle through the back door, nearly dragging the defiant James behind her.

I squeezed my way past an old deep-chest freezer and a child's plastic play house. Past the table of camping gear, tackle boxes, and hunting supplies, I found myself in front of the shelf. A few fishing poles and a shovel stood against it and I placed them on the table, accidentally knocking down a canvas satchel of hunting knives. Thankfully nothing broke (and I silently thanked all deities for no bloodshed on my part, despite my bad luck) as I gingerly placed them back on the table and proceeded with extra caution. All I needed was a giant spider to find me and my following freak-out would cause *me* to be buried alive in that garage.

Nearly twenty minutes later, I loaded up my

mother's bike with dry erase calendars, personal whiteboards, an array of bulletin board borders, flash cards, a few educational board games, and some office supplies. I frowned, realizing I wouldn't be able to carry the box of books with me and told Tammy I would come back for them soon.

"Okay, that's fine, doll," Tammy said, standing in the driveway with James wiggling around on her hip—he had refused to nap, apparently. "Thanks for taking it off my hands."

"No, thank you. This is a great haul," I said with my hands on the handle bars of the bike, ready to unload it at my mom's and take a closer look at my new goodies.

"Anytime, hun. I'll just keep the box of books in the garage, you come back when you can," Tammy informed me, trying to unclench James' hand from a lock of her hair.

"Thanks, Tammy." I waved and left her struggling to keep a hold on her squirmy two-year-old.

Almost immediately after I turned the corner, I ran into Carla who was hauling an old-fashion red wagon behind her. She worked at the pawn shop a door down from Prescott's and I assumed she was either making a delivery or adding it to the shop.

"Oh, Carla, I'm sorry," I said after nearly missing her on the bike. A few whiteboards slid out of the basket.

"No worries, Charli," she said. I got off the bike and extended the kick-stand to pick up the boards, but the weight of the teaching supplies caused the bike to fall over. The smaller items in the front basket tumbled into the grass as the rest of the whiteboards managed to slip out of the saddle bag pouch.

Drowning in newfound frustration, I groaned. "Here, let me help you," Carla offered, picking up a few items and placing them back in the basket.

"Thanks," I said a bit embarrassed. I moved the full saddlebag basket to the other side of the bicycle so it was more balanced.

"It's been a while since you were on a bicycle, huh?" Carla asked. I noticed her mood was lighter and it was beginning to lighten my suddenly sour disposition.

"Yeah," I admitted, sheepishly.

"Where are you coming from?" she asked, tossing a stapler-remover and a thick black permanent marker into the basket.

"Tammy's. She was giving away some of her old teaching supplies," I informed, collecting some magnets that had rolled into the dirt and placing them back into an old plastic butter container.

"Well that's nice. I'm glad she's keeping things together with everything that's been going on." I knew Carla was avoiding specific words and phrases and I was surprisingly glad she did; I guess I wasn't in the mood for any gossip.

"How is Cal doing? Did he decide on the University of Chicago?" I asked, trying to be friendly as I scanned the vicinity for any other items that had jumped ship.

Carla smiled. She was so proud of her son. "Oh, yes. We're driving up to Chicago next week for a tour. He's very excited."

"That's excellent. I'm so glad things are working out for him," I shared. I held the handlebars of the bike and released the kickstand.

"Yes, now they are," she said with an undertone I couldn't place. "Anyway, I have to get back to work. I'll see you around, Charli. Take care."

Stepping over the bike, I waved in her direction, wondering why the conversation felt so awkward. I shrugged it off as a nervous mother sending her son into the adult world and an extremely clumsy Alton. As a result, I carefully rode my mother's bicycle up Oak street, especially once it turned to a gravely dirt road, and was relieved when I finally reached the comforting presence of the Alton house.

CHAPTER 14

After three sweaty trips from the front lawn to my bedroom, I kicked off my shoes and collapsed on the threadbare throw rug on my bedroom floor. The occasional breeze was welcoming as it drifted lazily through the window. As I leisurely sifted through the goodies from Tammy, my cell phone vibrated off the nightstand and fell onto the floor beside me. Butterflies pummeled my stomach and I winced, hoping I wouldn't see Jackson's phone number on the bright screen. As I turned the phone over, I was glad when it indicated that my cousin, Jillian, was calling. Realizing that I was holding my breath, I let it out in relief. She was Jenna's twin sister and though we were ten years apart, I always used to pretend she was my big sister growing up.

"Jilli-Bean!" I exclaimed, answering the phone. I closed my eyes as a gust of wind rushed into the bedroom and I lifted my arms to erase the sweat. I crawled my way to the desk that housed my toiletries to apply a layer of deodorant that I had forgotten during my morning routine.

"Char-Berry!" Her tone matched mine and I loved hearing her nickname for me. She would take me to movies when I was in grade school and we'd always buy jelly beans and cherry-berry fruit snacks. It wasn't so much because we liked them, but because they sounded like our names.

"What are you doing right at this moment?" she asked. I could tell she was outside because the wind scraped across the line.

"Sorting through my booty," I said, sitting back down on the carpet, tossing old post-its into my office supplies pile.

"Too much information, dude," she said, jokingly. I laughed along with her and she continued, "I took the afternoon off. Meet me at The Grand Marquee in an hour. They're playing *Frozen Wet Feet*. My treat."

I squealed. *Frozen Wet Feet* was a cheesy '90's movie musical about dancing penguins in a magical world found in a picture frame at the main character's grandparent's house. I was one of the rare children who was in love with the movie and Jillian had taken me to see it at least a dozen times.

"No way!" I said. When was the last time I saw that movie? Goosebumps started to appear in anticipation and I got to my feet, looking for my shoes prematurely.

"Yes, way! I'm going home to change and then run a few errands. Meet me at 4:30 in front of the theatre?"

"A million times yes!" I hung up the phone excited to relive a relic from my childhood. It was a great distraction from the memories and issues I was avoiding.

Of course the movie was not as good as I remembered it being. Jillian and I walked out of the theatre in silent shock at how awful the movie really was. "Are you sure that was the same movie we saw in the nineties?" I asked as we were blinded by the sun, low in the western sky.

We sat down on one of the benches that lined Main Street. The Grand Marquee was located in the historic part of downtown so the street lamps, sidewalks, and landscaping were much more whimsical than the downtown on the other side of Oak Street. "I'm sure," Jillian confirmed. "I mean I remember it being bad, but not *that* bad."

"What? No," I said in disbelief. "You used to love that movie as much as I did. We saw it a billion times together."

Jillian shook her head with an empathetic smile, her curly brown hair danced in the slight breeze. "No, Char-Berry," she laughed. "I just went because you loved it so much."

The news surprised me and I melted a little inside realizing what my cool, older cousin did just to make me happy. "Well, that and I got a box of jelly beans out of it," she added.

I smiled at her. "Oh, yeah. Aunt Erin didn't like to let you eat sugar." Her mom was an anti-sugar brigadier before it was a thing, and every snack or meal was fruits, vegetables and seasoned meats.

"What she didn't know didn't hurt her," Jillian joked. I watched her gaze into the sunset, probably thinking about her mother. She still looked like my favorite cousin, but with a few years etched into her skin. A few gray hairs popped up at the roots on her temples and a faint pair of crows feet appeared when she smiled, but she still had that scar above her left eye and so much enthusiasm in her movements.

Pulling the opened bag of cherry-berry fruit snacks from my pocket, I dumped the last of them in my mouth and crumpled the wrapper in my hand, not yet ready to get up to throw it away. The plastic packaging crinkled in my fingers as we watched the sun dip lower behind the buildings in front of us.

As the shadow from the building began creeping up from our knees, Jillian said, "So I hear there's some crazy stuff happening around town."

"Oh, yeah, really crazy stuff," I agreed.

"Didn't get this much drama in Albuquerque, did you?" she asked, lightheartedly.

Suddenly, it was as if a shade was pulled from the

window of my memory, muting the light I was basking in moments ago. "Well," I said, my tone starkly different, "it was a different type of drama."

Jillian caught onto my tone. She shook a few jelly beans out of the box in her hands and popped them into her mouth. "I'm here if you need to talk about it," she offered.

I nodded. "I know." I blew my overgrown bangs from my eyes and scolded myself for not getting them cut yet. "Thank you."

She pulled her multi-colored bucket bag purse into her lap and fished around for a few moments before finally pulling out her keys. "Here," she said, handing me a key off the key ring. "In case you need a break from it all. I'm always at work, so if you need a quiet place, my cheese is sue's cheese." My face broke out into a smile and I laughed at the memories of a bad translation of *mi casa es su casa* from our childhood.

Still laughing, I said, "I love you, Jilli-Bean," and leaned over to give her a hug.

"Love you too, Char-Berry," she said, her breath smelling of fruity-flavored jelly beans.

Pulling apart, Jillian's tone turned conversational. "So I'm supposed to meet Jenna and Bailey for ice cream at Froz T's. Do you want to come?" Jillian asked, getting up from the bench. I threw the crinkling cherry-berry fruit snack packaging into the closest garbage can as two bicyclists went by on the street; their safety lights were flashing, despite the absence of night.

The theatre was squeezed between the drugstore and the police station. I automatically thought of Jake and realized it might be a good gesture to see if he wanted anything sweet to eat since he was buried under this case. "Sure. I want to stop in here first and see if Jake wants me to pick him up an ice cream taco or something. Meet you there?" I asked with my hand on the door knob.

Jillian nodded and waved, walking forward. "Later, Char-Berry."

Stepping into the station, a cloud of warmth billowed around me; it was almost stifling. I automatically unzipped my sweater as I once again greeted Seth at the front desk. He was filing papers in the cabinets behind him. "Back so soon, Charli?"

"Yeah, is Jake busy?" I asked, knowing that was a silly question. Who wasn't busy in this station with Sara's murder case?

"Probably. Go ahead back and see," he said, picking up another pile of papers from the desk. He was a lot less talkative than the last time I'd seen him and I took it as a sign that things around the Alton Oaks police station were getting serious.

Trying not to get in the way, I sashayed through the sea of bodies and chaos. Jake was sitting at his desk, his back to me. He was hunched over his work with the phone glued to his ear. His dark blonde hair was damp at the nape of his neck due to the temperature inside the station. The desk was covered in papers and folders that were half open and scattered among the swamp of post-its that littered his work area.

Hesitantly, I came into his line of view, hoping I wasn't being a bother. When he smiled and held up a finger that he'd be a moment more, I sat down at the chair beside his desk—it's faux brown leather padding ripped and covered in a strip of duct tape, a detail I hadn't noticed before.

I'm not intentionally nosy; it's just in my blood. It's a prerequisite for living in this town. It's how I was raised. At least, those were the excuses I told myself as my eyes skimmed over the papers he was studying. One in particular caught my eye and while Jake leaned over to copy something down in his Steno pad, I took the opportunity to get a closer look.

It was a sketch of a knife that looked like it was out of a supernatural TV show. It was shaped like a lighting bolt but the edges on one side were jagged, while the other side had a curved crescent moon blade near the handle. I was so enamored with studying it that I nearly jumped when Jake hung up the phone.

"Charli Parker, what brings you in today?" Jake asked, leaning back in his chair, his elbows on the arm rests and his fingers linked together. His eyes were tired and heavy but he still managed to force a twinkle to them. It was likely the first time he'd had a moment to take a break all day.

I cursed my Nordic heritage that made me blush so easily as I tried to cover up the fact that I was snooping. "Oh, well, I was about to head to Froz T's to meet up with Bailey, Jenna, and Jillian, and I know you've been busy, so I was just wondering if you wanted anything?"

A smile crept across his lips as I fidgeted. Finally, he said, "Any other time I'd say yes, but The Buzz just sent a variety of sugary caffeine treats over and I might have over done it." He glanced at his watch and said, "I'm due for a sugar crash in about an hour."

"All the more reason for ice cream," I said jokingly.

He smiled. "Thanks, Charli, but I'll take a rain check."

Just then another officer came to Jake's desk, ignoring me, and asked for a file. Swiveling in his chair, Jake shoved a few papers into a folder and handed it over.

"Busy?" I asked, wincing. I had noticed shadows forming under his eyes, which made him look much older.

He turned his head and raised his eyebrows at me.

"I know, stupid question," I replied, putting up my

hands in defense. "Can I get you anything? Did you eat?" I thought about the Oakies burrito he probably ate cold last night. "I can have Oakies deliver a burrito to you."

"I'm okay, Charli, really," he said between looking at me and clicking a program on his computer.

Giving in, I stood up and said, "All right, just let me know. I'll see you later, Jake."

He didn't say anything, but kept his attention on his computer, his hands flying over the keyboard.

But I couldn't go. I grudgingly plopped back down and sighed. Jake looked at me over his shoulder, amused. "Just can't tear yourself away, huh?" he joked.

"That," I said, pointing at the picture of the knife. "is bothering me. Is it from a sci-fi movie or something?"

Jake's lips briefly dipped into a frown, but in the end I guess he realized he could talk to me about it without revealing anything confidential. He picked it up and then shoved it closer to me. "It's a FoxLight brand hunting knife. Pretty unique in style. For serious hunters."

Looking up from the paper, I lifted an eyebrow and replied, "You're a serious hunter?"

Jake plucked the paper from my hand and tucked it into a folder. Smiling, he said, "I never said it was for me."

"It's turkey hunting season; I was just wondering. Bailey's husband, Carter, just went hunting but he only uses his turkey gun." I crossed my legs and leaned onto the desk as Jake started to copy something from the computer onto a yellow pad of paper.

"Yeah, FoxLight knives are expensive; not every hunter would have them," he said as a passing fact. "This is an older version, about twenty-years old."

"They're heavy and surprisingly sturdy," I said. I thought of the knives I'd dropped in Tammy's garage and must have had my guardian angel with me since I didn't get sliced. I had realized that that's where I saw that knife, and why it had bothered me so much.

"How do you know that?" he asked, only glancing from the computer to the pad of paper. "I didn't think you were much of a hunter."

"I saw them earlier today in a canvas carrying case. They're very impressive," I admitted, trying not to read the computer screen over his shoulder.

"Where was that?" Jake asked, turning his head to look at me, intensely interested in what I was about to say. He put the pencil down and surreptitiously leaned in closer to hear my answer.

"Tammy's garage. She was giving me some of her old teaching stuff and I knocked a bunch of knives off a table." I shrugged and didn't know where to look—it was hard to consciously not be snooping.

"Tammy?" Jake asked, searching my face for any more details. "Jim Browski's wife?"

I nodded, then it hit me. "Oh," I said in revelation. They were Jim's knives.

Jake automatically picked up his desk phone and started dialing.

CHAPTER 15

While Jake spoke on the phone and rummaged through files on his desk, I slunk out the front door. The cool air slid over my warm, damp skin, giving me the chills. Families were walking from the gardens outside Town Circle to their homes, a tradition many had when the weather was warm. A woman was adjusting the photography prints in the window of the art gallery across the street and two Canaries were tinkering with their bicycles outside the bike shop on the corner. Night had just fallen, but there was still a soft glow deep in the western sky. The air had adopted some humidity which chilled my lungs when I took a deep breath.

The realization that Jim really could be the murderer slapped me with stupidity as I stood there watching these clueless citizens mull about our historic downtown. He had the means, the motive, no alibi, and—most damning of all—the potential murder weapon. At least, I assumed it was the murder weapon with how Jake responded to our conversation.

I leaned against the lamp post as denial tried to take root. No. There's no way it was Jim. He must have been framed. It couldn't have been Jim. Not one of Alton Oaks' citizens. It's a misunderstanding. It just can't be true. Jim was the guy who ran the grocery store, who founded the Pineapple Bowl, who gave us our Thanksgiving turkeys. He couldn't have been the murderer...

The sound of teenagers on the corner, laughing and talking loudly as they walked north, stole my attention.

Jenna, Bailey, and Jillian were waiting for me in the distance at Froz T's. Not wanting to gossip or put on a happy face, I pulled out my cell phone and texted Jillian that I wouldn't be able to make it. Sure, it'd give Bailey fuel for rumors about Jake and me, but I didn't care. I needed a long, quiet walk to sort out my thoughts.

Turning left, instead of right, I decided to take Stony Drive to the elementary school and cut across my neighbors' backyards to get back home. I would avoid people that way. It was the route Sadie, Jake, and I took home when we were in fourth and fifth grade.

As the wind raced up from behind me, I zipped up my sweater and pulled the hood over my head. The promise of rain hung in the air as the tree branches danced in the distance. I cut behind Mr. Kratsky's workshop and all was quiet. The kitchen light poured into their backyard and I could pick up the faintest hint of roasted chicken in the air. About one hundred yards ahead, I could see Jillian's backyard glinting in the moonlight.

During the day, Jillian was a paralegal in the historic downtown district's Westbrook Attorney Office, wearing her high heels and a no-nonsense hair do, but at home, she walked barefoot in the garden, let her hair down, decorated in seashells, feathers, and crystals, and made an annual spiritual pilgrimage to Sedona, Arizona every June for a yoga retreat. She was engaged a few years out of high school, but a car accident had taken him away and left her with a scar above her left eye. Ever since, she's been a free soul who dances to the beat of her own music.

As I got closer to her house, I smiled seeing the Tibetan prayer flags and string of bronze bells dancing in the breeze on her back porch. It was too early to plant, but usually the air was pungent with herbs near her house, and the soil on the plot of land that would soon be a garden was turned and a wheel barrel was nearby.

Jillian's house was very peaceful with essential oils diffusing and binaural beats music playing throughout. It might just be what my soul needed. *Perhaps I will take her up on her offer,* I thought, fingering the house key she gave me that sat in my pocket.

After I crossed Gnarled Circle Drive, I saw Rip's house—it was still weird to say that. It was always the vacant house. The haunted house. The ghostly shadow we, for the most part, forgot about.

The echoing knock of a hammer bounded across the grass. At first, I almost cut left to Oak Street in order to avoid any type of interaction with Rip, but I grudgingly realized that in a town like Alton Oaks, it would be impossible. Besides, he was already an outsider; I might as well swallow my pride, be the bigger person, and apologize for my behavior.

Behind me the sky was painted in a deep purple and scarlet red, and the stars were beginning to poke through the horizon before me when I approached the house. Rip was on a ladder installing new screen canvas to the back porch. He had already made a lot of progress on the back end of the house. From my viewpoint, I saw that he'd already installed new stairs and a wooden frame where, I assumed, a screen door would be put in.

Rip wore a long-sleeved, dark blue, plaid flannel shirt that flapped in the breeze as he slipped the hammer into the loop on his black jeans and climbed down the ladder. He had utility spot lights cutting through the shadows that accompanied nightfall so he could continue to work. I could easily have walked past without being seen, as long as I avoided the spotlights—yes, the idea did cross my mind. Nonetheless, I swallowed my reservations and crossed into the light.

"Hey," I said, approaching the new back stairs. The wood had yet to be weather-proofed or painted and the smell of fresh cut wood hovered. Rip turned and crossed his hands over his chest, watching me invade his privacy. "Rip, right?" I asked.

He didn't respond, but looked down at me, his gelled hair now falling out of place and onto his face. A dramatically loud breath escaped his lips which, I think, held back the words no one would be happy to hear.

I stuffed my hands deeper into my pockets and tried not to avoid eye contact, but I wasn't very successful. My eyes traveled across the tall grass, the oak trees ahead, my shoes. "I wanted to apologize for my behavior the other day," I choked out, balling my hands into fists.

After a few unsettling moments, he bent down to grab his red metal toolbox. "Do you always trespass on other people's property?" he asked, brushing past and setting the toolbox on the top of the stairs.

I hesitated to say anything for a few moments. The bright lights felt like x-ray machines, trying to unravel the layers inside me. It made me very uncomfortable. "Sorry," I finally mumbled and decided the best course of action was to abandon ship. I turned to continue my trek home, slipping easily into the shadows once again.

The wind had picked up and the air grew heavier with the smell of rain. We were in for a storm, so I picked up my pace, practically sprinting across Jenna's yard. I didn't look back until I reached my parents' front porch. I was never going to figure that man out.

Not long after I'd helped put the dinner dishes away, and Dad had walked in the door, the storm began. When the storm got worse, our shadows moved from burning light bulb to burning light bulb. Mom, Dad, and

I began running through the house hastily patching up holes with plastic canvas, emptying old buckets, and putting out new buckets. Our silhouettes rushed back and forth as the wind rattled the windows and the garage door continually banged open against the frame.

The house creaked in its foundation and I realized it was in worse shape than I'd remembered. The north end of the living room was the worst and the winds kept tearing down the plastic that was stapled to the rotting wood. The sleeves and front of my sweater were thoroughly soaked by the time the storm had dissipated to a spring shower.

After a hot shower, I crawled into my bed, listening to the rain drops on the roof and the rain leaking into the bucket near my window. A musty smell clung to the air and I pulled the quilt tighter around me for warmth.

Storms lull me right to sleep, thunder or no thunder. I could sleep through the fiercest ones.

I woke up in the middle of the night when the lightning was dying down and the rain was so light I couldn't hear it anymore. It misted against my bedroom window while the shadows of trees swayed into my bedroom. It was odd for me because I always slept through the night; I wasn't one to wake up in the middle of the night without a reason. Ever. For a few moments I sat there, waiting to go back to sleep; letting my deep breathing act as a lullaby when I heard no foreign noises or movements in my room... no reason to be awake.

Then my phone vibrated. The screen lit up momentarily, scaring away the shadows that slumbered on my bedside table. I picked it up and squeezed my eyes shut a few times and squinted until I could read the screen. It was a voicemail and a missed call from Jackson.

Jackson. My husband.

I sighed and rolled over. I didn't want to deal with that right now. My thoughts were a dust storm and I couldn't even begin to go over them until it all settled. Just the thought of having to talk to him again made my stomach wring like a sponge.

Did I want him back? No...not at this moment, at least. Would that change? I didn't know; only time would tell, I guessed. But what he did hurt, stabbed deeply into my heart.

Stabbed.

Oh, poor Sara. She'd had her whole life ahead of her. And it ended too early on the dirty floor of a backroom in a supermarket. Who would do that? Who *could* do that? Was Jim really capable of it? One of our very own Alton Oaks residents? He had the means, he had the motive, but did he have the opportunity? He didn't have much of an alibi, but the possibility of an Alton Oaks resident committing murder was hard to swallow.

But then again, the steamy letters he wrote to Sara, who was underage, could have been used as blackmail. No one expected him to be capable of that either, or, at least, I didn't.

And I didn't exactly trust Rip; he had his defenses up about something. He was there that night, a stranger in town talking to a seventeen-year-old grocery clerk in a dark alleyway. There was the lighter with his fingerprints. Of course, Sara could have just pocketed it after borrowing it from Rip to light a cigarette. Or maybe Sara invited him inside the store and he misplaced it. Or, worse yet, perhaps he dropped it while terrorizing her and, ultimately, taking her life.

Rip made goose bumps raise on my arms regardless.

And then their was Cal. No one ever expects the good boy with the alibi.

Groaning, I tore the blankets from my bed, realizing

that I wasn't going back to sleep. In my sweatpants and old EIU hoodie, I slipped my feet into a pair of shoes and crept downstairs. As I tip-toed past the Grandfather clock at the bottom of the stairs, its pendulum swinging carelessly into the night, I realized that the sun would rise soon.

Raiding my father's stash of coffee, I began brewing a cup while I walked around the first floor inspecting water damage and throwing the rain water from filled buckets out the windows. Before long, I was walking onto the front porch with an old comforter to keep me warm, an extra large mug of coffee to keep me awake, and my tablet to check in with life outside of Alton Oaks.

The porch swing was my favorite place in the world. It was where Mom had taught me to read, where I'd gotten my first kiss, and it was where my family was during the bearable months of the year. My dad would bring his small television outside to watch baseball games, and my brother, Alex, would use chalk to create mazes for Bailey and me to wander through, and Sadie and I spent many middle school sleepovers in the summer camped out on the porch swing.

Sighing with nostalgia, I immediately got comfortable by wrapping myself in the comforter. Smelling the scent of my mother's fabric softener made me feel safe. As I inhaled the intoxicating scent of petrichor, everything seemed a bit greener outside. Even the annual tulips that grew on either side of the stairs were beginning to pop up. Happily, I swung my legs up beside me, held the warm mug in my lap, and began to check my email.

As I answered emails and navigated through social media, I saw postings from friends and old co-workers. The third grade teacher's retirement party—I'd forgotten about that. I scrolled through photos of the school's field day and longed to give hugs and high fives to my students. At least they looked happy.

Putting the tablet down for a moment, I stared into the oak trees, watching a squirrel jump from branch to branch. Its movements unleashed a flurry of raindrops that had collected during the night and were waiting to dry in the morning sun. I began to doubt whether moving back to Illinois had been the right choice. That cozy feeling that greeted me only minutes ago was just a memory as I bit my lip and battled thoughts in my head while looking distractedly into the distance.

Just as the sun began to rise behind the house and cast long shadows down Oak Street, I heard my dad rummaging around in the kitchen. Today was his scheduled day off, but that wouldn't stop him from popping into Oakies and finding work to do, even if it was just to socialize with the customers. My dad was a bit of a workaholic, but at least he loved his work.

The morning dew and leftover raindrops licked the grass that was due for a mowing. I shivered thinking about how cold my toes would get walking through it this morning. A young boy came riding up Oak Street, throwing the latest issue of *The Oak Leaf Press* onto the porches. The scene made me smile because in New Mexico it was an adult in a car driving through the street at three in the morning, throwing newspapers from his car window (that never ended up near the front doors). The boy politely waved and said, "Morning," as he tossed the bundle to the top of the stairs and then made his way back down the street.

The smell of bacon wafted through the kitchen window and caught on the light breeze. I was about to gather my belongings and wander inside when I saw Rip wandering into our yard from Jenna's. Curious, I got up from the swing and stood at the top of the stairs, leaning against the beam, and watched him approach the house.

"Do *you* always trespass on *your* neighbor's property?" I asked, hiding a smirk and mocking his comment from yesterday.

He was in a pair of white painting paints and a dark blue t-shirt that was splattered with paint. His shoes, and the pants above his ankles were wet from the soggy grass he'd crossed. He wore a baseball cap that sat backwards on his head. It pulled the hair from his face to reveal the startling comfort in his chocolate-brown eyes, which brought out the dark stubble on his chin and cheeks. Stopping at the bottom of the stairs, he let the gallon of paint he'd been carrying rest three steps from my feet.

"Look," he began, taking off his hat and running a hand through his hair, "I'm not used to this so just shut up and let me do this." He replaced the cap and sighed. Before speaking again, he nudged the gallon of paint with his foot. "Peace offerin'. I'm not good at fixin' first impressions, but I figure since everyone thinks I'm a murderer anyway, I can't do any worse."

"So you brought paint?" I asked, descending the stairs and picking it up. "Not even a full gallon?"

Rip shrugged exaggeratedly by putting his palms into the air. "I don't have anything. It was this, some rotted wood, or some horrible, day old egg rolls from a Chinese place east of Terryville." He paused. "Or not come at all."

"Well, then," I started, looking down from the step I was on, "at least you're not completely full of bad choices."

Rip let a small smile escape and it disappeared as quickly as it came. I heard the rusty hinges on the screen door screech and turned to see my dad with an apron on over his pajamas and an oven mitt on his left hand. "Breakfast is ready—" my dad said then stopped when he saw Rip.

Before I even thought about making an introduction, my dad walked down the porch stairs in his rubber-soled slippers and extended a hand. "Rip, nice to see you again. How's the house coming along?"

My dad stood on the stair beside me, and the smell of maple syrup and bacon he carried with him made my stomach rumble. "Not bad. Nearly finished the back porch, but the rain last night—man, it was rough. So I painted the kitchen. Roofers are coming on Thursday and the contractors are coming week after next."

Nodding, my dad added, "Don't forget about getting permits. My brother-in-law is the mayor, lives next door with my niece and her husband." He turned to me and added, "Maybe Charli can introduce you sometime?"

They both looked at me like they forgot I was standing there. "Yeah... sure," I said, swatting away the topic at hand and wanting a question answered. "How do you know each other?"

"Rip comes into the restaurant all the time. He's working his way through the red meat portion of the menu." My dad shrugged as if it was common knowledge.

"And the beers of the world," Rip added with a nod.

My dad smiled in recognition and then offered, "You're welcome to stay for breakfast."

Rip hesitated. He took off his hat, ran a hand over his hair again and then replaced the hat. "Nah, been up all night painting. Some other time," he replied.

As Rip walked away, I discreetly said to my dad as we walked up the stairs, "You do know the whole town thinks he's a murderer, right?"

Grabbing the screen door and letting me inside, he responded, "Well, it's a good thing I don't think like the town." As we walked through the dining room, he added, "He's just different. Sometimes the people here need a while to get used to newbies." My dad didn't grow up in Alton Oaks, so I had to believe he knew what it was like to be an outsider in our town.

I placed the gallon of paint onto the dining room table as Dad disappeared into the kitchen. Glancing out the window I saw Rip walking across the grass. He disappeared behind Jenna's house and I wondered who he really was. Why had he chosen Alton Oaks? Why that house?

CHAPTER 16

"So, according to Carter, Eli was standing in the grass." Mom was buttering her five grain toast with coconut butter as we sat around the breakfast table listening to her share a story about Eli's first turkey hunt. Dad and I exchanged glances as we took bites of our syrup-drenched pancakes and listened. "Carter was teaching him to be really quiet so Eli's tip-toeing through the grass. Then suddenly this big fat one jumps up out of nowhere and Eli goes crashing—"

Mom was cut off by the sound of Mrs. Kratsky's *hee-haw, hee-haw* horn. We could just hear the crunching of gravel beneath the golf cart's tires as she pulled into our driveway. Mom turned her head and, like an animal of prey who'd heard a noise, listened intently for another whisper. The rubber soles of Mrs. Kratsky's slip-on shoes were heard climbing up the creaking front stairs. In a flash, Mom wiped her face with a napkin and went to meet her on the porch. There must be some big news rolling around Alton Oaks this early morning.

My dad rolled his eyes at her need for gossip. Mom and Dad were very different that way; he was definitely not an Alton, *and* he grew up in Sheridan. Mom shot through the front door before we could say anything about missing breakfast. Dad looked up from the morning edition of *The Oak Leaf Press* and stole the last piece of bacon from Mom's plate and gave me a wink—until he realized it was soy bacon which he spit out into a napkin, dramatically. "I guess I deserved that," he admitted, wiping his tongue with the napkin.

I laughed before returning to my pile of pancakes. It was such a comforting scene that it made me sure that moving back to Illinois was the right thing to do.

Dad began to clear the plates from the table and I interjected, "I got it, Daddy. You go do something fun." He gave me a smile, but we both knew he was clueless as to what to do. Oakies was his life. "You can go visit Bailey. I'm sure Eli will keep you busy. Maybe you can hear the end of Eli's first turkey hunting trip."

He kissed me on the top of my head as I began to wash the dishes in the deep porcelain basin. "Actually, I'm going to your brother's house. He needs help with some home improvement projects."

My head whipped to where he was standing in the archway, one hand holding a bottle of yellow dish soap and the other gripping the funny-smelling sponge. "Alex?" My tone verged between excitement and anxiousness and I soon regretted the offer to clean up the kitchen. "I want to visit!"

My older brother is a physician at the hospital. He was always busy and worked odd hours. He just bought a house a year or two ago on the same block as Sadie's apartment. Alex and I used to be very close. In fact, he inspired me to join the Peace Corps since he always talked about doing the Doctors Without Borders program. But after I eloped with Jackson, Alex and I lost touch. I know he didn't really like my husband, but I chose my marriage over my family.

"Come on by after you get off Cinderella duty," Dad joked. His tone turned sincere when he added, "Alex would really like to see you."

Smiling, I agreed and focused on finishing the dishes and cleaning the sticky drops of syrup, dusting of pancake mix, and splattering of oil from the kitchen surfaces.

Nearly an hour later, when the last dish was put away, the counters gleamed in squeaky cleanliness and not a speck of dust nor flour hid in the corners and crevices of the kitchen, I dug out a pair of rubber boots from the front hall closet and grabbed my sweater which I'd draped on the banister. I was excited and nervous about seeing Alex again. Would he be stand-offish because I chose Jackson? Would he say, "I told you so," and rub it in that he was right about Jackson all along? Would he ignore me—or worse—be angry with me when I showed up on his doorstep? No matter what was going to happen, he was my big brother and I missed him. I hoped we could get back our relationship.

Walking outside, the leftover puddles and raindrops seemed to magnify the sunshine. I squinted, making out the trail Mrs. Kratsky's wheels had left on the overgrown grass in our yard. To my right, Mrs. Kratsky and my mom had their heads together, talking fervently about something as they sat hunched over the bench on the front porch. I guess the lead Jake had gotten last night about the knife had led to something. Looking between Oak Street and the gossiping ladies on the porch, I was torn. When did the yearning for news become such a weak spot for me?

I let the screen door slap the frame behind me, allowing the rusted hinges to moan in defiance. Both heads snapped my way. "Charli! Did you hear?" Mrs. Kratsky asked, her face glowing and her spirit bubbling. She waved for me to come closer and I gave in.

Shaking my head, I sat down on the bench beside them. "What happened? Is everyone okay?" I asked.

Mrs. Kratsky shook her head animatedly. "Jim Browski was arrested last night. During the peak of the storm." She talked as if she wished she could have been there.

My thoughts shot back to the sketch of the knife at

the police station. "Arrested?" I asked. My eyebrows dipped at the realization that Jim was probably the murderer, the one who did those horrible, unspeakable things to Sara.

She nodded. "Apparently, they found the murder weapon in his garage—just out there in the open, not even hidden." She slapped her knee, giddy with the news. "Like he was boasting about it."

"It was really him? It was really the murder weapon?" I asked, shock tensing my shoulders.

Mrs. Kratsky nodded. "It was a FoxLight hunting knife. They found blood on the handle. Haven't proved it was really Sara's blood, but it's pretty damning evidence, isn't it?"

I chose my words carefully. "I don't know. They found blood on a hunting knife. Isn't it more likely it's animal blood?" I asked. "I mean Jim Browski can't be guilty. He played basketball with Alex in high school. Could he have had it in him to kill the entire time?"

Mom put a hand on my shoulder. No one wanted to admit that he had the ability to commit murder; it was too close to home. The evidence, however, was pretty damning. Shivering, I zippered my jacket.

"They must have gotten a tip," my mom explained to Mrs. Kratsky, dismissing my skepticism, "because they started with the garage instead of the house." After a few moments of birds chirping and the wooden rocking chair creaking with the breeze, my mother turned to me and asked, "Didn't you go to Jim's house the other day? For some teaching supplies or something?"

Mrs. Kratsky's eyes widened and focused on me. "Really?" she asked.

This is my penance for choosing to stay for gossip instead of going straight to Alex's, I thought to myself before answering the question. "Yeah," I admitted. Both women's eyes continued to search me for new information.

"Charli!" my mother gasped. "It was you." She held her hand to her heart like I had committed a sin.

Closing my eyes and wrinkling my brow, I condemned myself for not going straight to Alex's house. "Maybe," I admitted. "Kinda, sorta," I added and opened my eyes. "Yeah."

"Charlotte May Parker!" my mother scolded. She stuttered at a loss of words. "Why don't you tell me these things?" she finally asked.

Only shrugging, I winced and said, "I don't know." I was getting flashbacks from when I was a child and got yelled at for fighting with Bailey. I half expected my mother to send me to my room.

"Oh, Charli," Mrs. Kratsky interjected. "Your tip caused quite the show. Your boyfriend hauled Jim away in the rain last night—lightning flashing and all—like it was a TV show," Mrs. Kratsky added, gesturing towards me, nearly bouncing in her seat.

Rolling my eyes at her comment was all I could do. Since the third grade everyone teased me that Jake was my boyfriend since he was one of my best friends. When we got to high school and grew apart, then they nitpicked me about *not* having a boyfriend. When I met Jackson, they constantly sighed and made not-so-hidden comments about how I could do better. There was just no pleasing my family.

"Where did you hear all this?" I asked, trying to avoid my mother's eyes. Usually I took what they discussed with a grain of salt because some of it was true and some of it was rumors. This story seemed to be legitimate.

"*Everyone* is talking about it," Mrs. Kratsky said and took a sip from her to-go coffee cup. "Mr. K. and I went to The Buzz this morning like we do every Sunday and the place was *abuzz* with the news." She sighed. "Sometimes it's a curse living this far from town."

Mom nodded, but didn't say anything. She shot me a look from the corner of her eye.

Mrs. Kratsky continued, "I heard the story from Bonnie Lipinski—she's the principal of the junior high now, did you know? She lives on the corner of Oak and Sheridan, right next to Jim and Tammy's. She said she saw the whole thing from her kitchen window," Mrs. Kratsky finished. "Tammy's so torn up about it, she wants to leave town. Bonnie saw her packing boxes early this morning."

"Wow," was all I could say as I stared at my feet. After a few moments I looked up and asked, "Do you really think he did it?"

My mother chewed on the question. She shrugged and nodded her head giving me mixed signals. I was relieved she was communicating with me without glares and heart-breaking glances.

"Sure does look like it, huh?" Mrs. Kratsky said, finishing off her coffee. "Looks like he and Sara wrote those letters to each other, and Sara must have threatened him with blackmail, or wanted to go public or something, and he snapped. He killed her that night, tried to wash away the blood and put the knife back like nothing happened." She sniffed and added, "Hope he gets what he deserves."

Feeling as though that was all the news they had to share, and Mom wouldn't get too mad if I left, I stood up. "I'm heading to Alex's; let me know if you guys hear anything more, okay?"

Mrs. Kratsky said with enthusiasm, "You got it."

Mom nodded and added stonily, "You do the same."

I forced a smile as I realized I was still in hot water.

The news was still swimming in my head as my boots sunk and sucked in and out of the muddy road on our side of town. The road was only paved on the west side of US-16, where the cemetery ended and the schools started popping up. Questions, doubts, and accusations about the entire case invaded my thoughts, poisoning them like an epidemic.

Cutting through Main Street, I traveled through the cars sitting in the parking lot of late brunchers at Oakies. Alex's new house was right behind Dad's restaurant and I wondered if that brought them closer.

It was a two-story house with white siding. Freshly painted blue wooden stairs led up to the porchless entry. It was quaint with rose bushes crawling up lattice on either side of the stairs and a pot of blue flowers hung from the awning to the right of the door. It looked like it had a woman's touch and I wondered if Alex was seeing anyone.

Wiping my muddy boots on the plain black rubber welcome mat, I felt a pang of anxiety tear through my body. I so wished to be close with Alex again, but wondered if our relationship could ever be the same. He was always my protective big brother; my superhero. I missed that.

The storm door was open and I could hear voices carrying through the screen door. I knocked and wondered if I should take off my boots before I walked in; they were caked in mud, and dried flecks of it were coming off as the sun dried out the town.

When I looked up from inspecting my boots, Alex stood on the other side of the screen. He was a whole head taller than me and looked down through his wire rimmed glasses. He was still lanky, but had filled out a bit, making him seem older; the way he moved and carried himself was full of maturity.

"Hi, Alex," I said meekly, looking up at him through the screen.

Almost immediately, a smile grew across his face

and he opened the door, which didn't screech in protest. "Charli," he said, embracing me in a hug, picking me up from the floor. "Welcome home," he said, placing me in his foyer.

I clung to his dark brown sweater that smelled like Mom's brand of fabric softener, holding back tears. I didn't realize it until that moment, but Alex was the person I feared most to see coming back home because, growing up, I had always looked so highly upon his opinion. Relief washed over me when he welcomed me back with a hug that held no hesitation.

"Thanks, Alex," I said through his shirt. It was all we needed to say to each other.

When we parted, Dad stood behind him and I was suddenly struck by how much they looked alike. They could pass for brothers, except that my dad's messy brown hair was shorter and peppered in gray, especially at his temples. "You made it just in time, Charlotte May I," my dad said. "You can help hold up the two-by-fours."

"Two-by-fours?" I asked. "For what?"

Alex led me through the living room and into the kitchen where the back door stood wide open, letting fresh chilly air fill the warm house. "We're rebuilding the back stairs," Alex said. "We put in the back patio in October, and I'm tired of having to go out the front door to get to the garage."

Looking down over the progress they'd made, I could see they had cemented in support beams prior to today and cut the overgrown grass. "When Dad said you were doing a home improvement project I kinda thought it was installing bookshelves or mounting a TV," I said, surveying the patio.

And then there was Sadie, at the table saw below the young oak tree, wearing a pair of overalls and safety glasses, cutting a portion of wood.

As the cut piece fell into the soggy grass, she cut the power to the saw, making the backyard fall silent. "Sadie! What are you doing here?" I asked, wishing I could jump over the mess of wood and give her a hug. It might have only been two days since I'd last seen her, but she was my life jacket. How did I make it all those years with only our phone calls and sporadic visits?

"Alex needed a table saw, and you know how I feel about lending out my power tools," she said, carrying the cut board to a pile of prepared lumber.

Sadie had control issues. Her dad was a lawyer, and her mom was a woodworking artist. Her mom had had their garage transformed into a workshop where she made beautiful furniture that she sold at the swamp markets and high end resale shops as far away as Springfield. She taught Sadie a lot and when her parents moved to Florida, Sadie kept all the tools in a storage shed.

"It's good that you're here," Sadie said in a no-nonsense tone. She set down the board in a pile of similar cut wood and took off a pair of gloves. "Cause I gotta go run to Davenport and these *men*," she said the word while rolling her eyes like it was a chore, "need some direction."

"Hey! We took down the old staircase last summer without you," Alex said playfully as he jumped down into the backyard.

"Oh yay; you destroyed something. What a challenge," she said, unimpressed.

"You," Sadie said, pointing at me and catching my gaze, "are in charge of making sure *no one* touches my tools." Below me, Dad made a grunting sound when he had climbed down from the patio, following Alex into the yard.

"You're trusting me with your tools?" I asked, gripping the wooden ledge above where the staircase should be. After our twenty-plus year friendship, we had reached a huge milestone where she trusted me with her tools—it was a big step! Even in the Kindergarten sandbox, she wouldn't share her glitter-encrusted purple shovel.

"Not to use," Sadie clarified, a little too forcefully. She came up right below me and in a softer voice explained, "These are my babies, Charli. You make sure they are not touched, abused, or even looked at for too long. I will be back in a few hours."

With my hand to my forehead, I saluted her. "Aye, aye, captain."

Sadie squinted and then shielded her eyes with her hand, almost saluting me back. "I trust you, Charli," she said more for her benefit than for mine.

"Peace out, boys," Sadie said, throwing her gloves onto the table saw and making her way down the gangway.

"What a pistol," Dad said as we watched her exit.

"Mm-hm," Alex agreed as I climbed down from the patio without their assistance.

"Okay," I said, ignoring my father's comment and turned to face Alex and Dad. "What do we do now?"

For a moment we were clueless. Dad sorted through the pile of wood and Alex scratched his head. "I think it goes like this," I said, putting two boards in place.

"Oh, then this goes here," my dad added, pulling another piece of wood from Sadie's pile.

"Shoot," my brother added after we picked up a rhythm. "Sadie made this easy," he said, picking up a can of nails that sat on the cement walkway.

"Let's do this!" I said, excited to work between my brother and father.

As we carried the first board over, Alex held the stair stringers in place and asked, "So how are things at work?"

I handed my dad a nail as he secured the stringer to the porch and replied, "It's great. We just hired a new cook. Brett Dennison—know him? He went to culinary school in Chicago and married a local, Tiffany something." He opened his palm for another nail which I delivered. "He works well with Oscar; they're developing a new menu for the fall. We're looking into getting locally grown produce—apparently it's all the rage now," he shared.

"Won't people be upset if the menu changes?" I asked. I liked how I could depend on its predictability no matter how long I was absent from town.

"That's the good thing," my dad explained between pounding the hammer. "We keep the same menu, but the ingredients change—higher quality. Oscar threw around the idea of having a dish two ways—old way and new—but we're not sure it will fit in the budget. We're still hammering out the details," Dad added and then wiggled his eyebrows. "Get it?" he asked, looking from me to Alex. "Hammering out the details?" he said while waving the hammer in his hands.

Alex and I exchanged looks and groaned at his joke.

Taking the level, Alex checked the stringer to be sure it was straight before Dad secured the other end. Dad crouched down, ready to start hammering when he got Alex's approval. "How are things with you and—" Dad said, but was cut off much too quickly by Alex.

"Work is excellent. Always busy, you know," he said almost stuttering. "Hey, Charli," he said, changing the subject, "What have you been up to since you got back home? Hanging out with Sadie a lot?"

Oblivious to any awkwardness, I answered, "Oh some. She's busy with work. Mainly I've been talking to Jake Vega a lot."

My dad started hammering and Alex smiled. "Oh, I remember him. You guys used to sit on the porch stairs and wait for Sadie before walking to school. I didn't know you kept in touch with him."

Handing my dad another nail, I replied, "We didn't, really. Our paths just keep crossing with this whole murder case. I seem to always be in the wrong place at the wrong time."

With a smile, he commented, "Ah, that's the Charli I know."

For the rest of the morning and well into the afternoon, we installed the back stairs—mostly through trial-and-error—and were confident enough in our handyman skills to sit on them when we finished. As the heat of the day waned, we drank cans of soda and talked and laughed with the ball game on the radio in the background. It was refreshing, for a change, to not have my mind riddled with details of a murder, a list of suspects, and the life I'd left behind in New Mexico.

CHAPTER 17

"Who's up for some burgers?" my dad asked as he wiped the sweat from his forehead and onto his sleeve. The work we had done, mixed with the humid day, caused us all to sweat a bit.

"Yes!" Alex agreed as he swept the saw dust and loose nails from the sidewalk.

"And milk shakes!" I said from the ground where I held a dustpan for Alex.

"Great!" Dad said, walking towards the back gate. "I'll run to Oakies. Don't work too hard," he added a little too excited to find an excuse to visit work.

As soon as Dad closed the gate behind him, Alex and I collapsed into the folding chairs in front of the staircase. "Probably not worth the effort to open the can of sealant right now," Alex said.

"Just to close it up again when lunch gets here," I added, completely on the same page as my brother.

A gentle breeze floated into the yard and rocked the buds growing on the lilacs behind Alex. "Pretty cool house, Alex," I said, resting my ankle on my opposite knee. "Still hard to believe you're a grown up."

Alex kicked my foot off my ankle from where he sat. "I'm not the only one growing old," he said and adjusted his glasses. "Bailey made our parents grandparents."

"And she's younger than both of us!" I exclaimed.

Alex smiled and let it fade from his face. "Listen," Alex said, leaning forward in his chair, his tone turning serious. "Since it's just us, I just want to say I'm sorry about," he hesitated for a moment, "about what you're going through."

I turned in my chair and opened my mouth to wave away the subject before the discussion became something I wasn't ready for.

"No." Alex stopped me. His chair made a short metal screech as he dipped his gaze towards his feet. "It can't be easy, what you're going through. You're good at hiding it; you never want other people to worry about you."

I bit my lip as I watched him talk. He picked up a small twig and scraped it against the sidewalk. "I never liked Jackson. I don't think that was a secret." He briefly looked up at me and then he continued drawing invisible pictures with the stick. "I didn't like him because I didn't think he deserved you. It drove us apart—you and me—and I know it was because of me. I wasn't there for you when you needed me, but at least you had Sadie."

"Alex," I started again, hoping he'd let me continue. He put up his hand and looked up at me.

"I promise not to meddle again and if you ever need anything, I'll be here. I'll always be here for my little Charli May," he said and smiled. He reached over and rubbed my head with his fist for a half-hearted noogie.

I blinked away the tears that were forming behind my eyelids and smiled. He didn't approach me with questions or rumors and I couldn't have been more grateful. "Thanks, Alex," I said, swatting away his hand.

"I mean it," he reiterated. "Don't let anyone make you feel like you're not worth fighting for."

I leaned over and gave him a hug. "I've missed you," I admitted.

"Same here, Charli May," he said, poking me in the ribs.

After a few moments of listening to the sounds of downtown travel past the line of oak trees and into the backyard, I asked, "What have you been up to, Alex? Not just work—don't give me that," I said, raising a finger. "Are you seeing anyone?" I asked.

Alex unexpectedly laughed and emptied his can of coke. "Why would you ask that?"

"Because your house is gorgeous; it has a woman's touch. And I know you. In college you used cinder blocks and a piece of warped plywood as a coffee table. Don't think I didn't notice that your plates matched your mugs when I walked through your kitchen."

"Lunch is here!" Dad's voice traveled over the back gate before we could continue our conversation. "If you want a milkshake, you have to let me in," he said, laden down with Oakies' take-out bags, and kicked the gate with his foot. Alex jumped up from his seat eagerly and much too quickly to let Dad into the backyard. Our conversation faded with the coming of burgers, crinkled fries, and cold, frosty milkshakes.

After we stuffed ourselves with a hearty Oakies meal, we waterproofed the wooden case of stairs in Alex's backyard with a sealant. Sadie stopped by in the evening with her pick-up truck and to put her tools back in storage.

"How are my babies?" Sadie asked, walking into the backyard. She went straight for the tools that nobody had touched and ignored us.

"We're just fine, darling," I replied, jokingly. Alex nearly spit out his soda at my comment which gave me a confidence boost. I always loved making him laugh.

Sadie rolled her eyes and gave her tools a once-over. "No one touched them, I swear," I reported from the folding chair I had parked myself in an hour ago.

Happy with the state of her power tools, Sadie

walked over to the circle our three chairs made with a TV tray in the middle. Without hesitating, Sadie sat in my lap and grabbed a handful of potato chips from the bag on the table. She was still wearing her overalls and a paint-splattered t-shirt. She had taken off her red flannel shirt and tied it around her waist while she was gone. "Looks good, boys," Sadie commented, looking over at the staircase. "Was anyone brave enough to walk up them?" she asked with a laugh.

"We sat on them," Alex said, proudly.

Sadie turned to look at me for a report. "All three of us did," I agreed with my brother.

Hiding a smile, Sadie got up from my lap and brushed the residue from her snack off her hands. "Do you wanna help me load the truck? Then we can leave these boys to see what's playing at the Grand Marquee. My treat?" she asked, holding out a hand.

Taking her hand, she pulled me out of the chair. "Done and done," I said.

"That's a sweet deal," my dad commented, finishing off his can of soda.

"Yeah," my brother chimed in. "How do we get in on this?"

Sadie chewed on an idea while I brushed crumbs from my Oakies meal off my lap. "If you boys are gentlemanly enough to help me load the truck, Monday morning's coffees are on me."

Alex shot up faster than I expected. I guess when you work eighteen-hour shifts, you need all the caffeine you can get.

After I'd helped Sadie unload her tools into the storage shed she rents from Mrs. Flanagan, her landlord, she dropped me off at the Alton House. We planned to meet on the corner of Stony and Sheridan in an hour so she could drop her car off, we could change our clothes, and grab a bite to eat.

Back on Main Street, the town was still buzzing about what had happened to Jim Browski. The few hours at Alex's was a nice reprieve from the anxiety, fear, and gossip, but now I was back in Alton Oaks proper. So, of course, I decided to go out of my way an extra block and reach my destination by walking past Jim's house, because my mom's blood runs through my veins.

Just as I reached Sheridan Avenue, I immediately ran into Allyson, a girl from high school who used to be on the volleyball team with Sadie and me. She was walking behind a baby blue stroller with a blanket draped over it to hide the baby's face. Her peppy personality was evident in her step and she smiled brightly when she saw me.

"Charli Parker! I haven't seen you in years." She walked around the stroller, her long blonde hair swaying over her shoulders.

It took me a few moments to remember her name, but it came to me as we released the obligatory hug of small town nostalgia. "Hi, Allyson. You look good. What have you been up to?"

She gripped the stroller and rocked it back and forth as she talked. "Thanks, Charli. I hear you've done some great things since high school. The Peace Corps? Awesome. Josh and I got married—do you remember Josh Perkins from high school?—and we moved back to Alton Oaks a few years ago. Just had Blake here in the summer," she said, motioning towards the stroller, then readjusted the blanket. I couldn't squeeze a word in, so I let her talk. "I almost forgot you were back in town. So much has happened. Can you believe what happened to Jim? It's horrible. I used to think of Alton Oaks as a modern day, edgier version of Mayberry, but I guess we've caught up to the rest of the world."

I nodded, following her train of words and wondered if I'd be late to meet Sadie. "Have you heard anything new since the arrest?" Allyson asked, fishing for new gossip.

"Nah," I said, waving my hand. "It's a shame though. I can't believe it was Jim. He never seemed to be capable of anything like that."

Allyson nodded, agreeing. "Josh and I bought the house next door to them. I could hardly believe it when I saw the police lights in the rain last night. My older boy, Liam—he's three, plays with their son, James. Poor Tammy, too. I can't imagine what she's going through. He has a set of lungs on him, that James." She widened her eyes to exaggerate. "That boy can scream. And to think the night that Jim was killing Sara, James cried like he had colic. The poor boy screamed and screamed for a good hour, hour and a half. Lights on all night. I finally got to sleep when he quieted around 11:30. Maybe he knew something we didn't. Kids are like that, you know. Did you end up having any?"

I bit my lip before I answered so that I didn't say anything I didn't want to. My goal was to not overshare even though Allyson had a personality that made me want to spill information. "No. No kids. I'm a teacher; the students are my kids."

"Yeah. I remember when you got married. Shocked the whole town. Eloped in Vegas, right?" Allyson wiggled her eyebrows playfully. "Scandalous!"

Allyson would have loved for me to tell her the whole story about how I met Jackson and why we married in Vegas, but I couldn't. "It was good catching up with you, Allyson. I'd love to chat longer, but I'm supposed to meet Sadie for a movie. We'll talk later?"

Allyson frowned for a split second, but her face lit up when she shared, "Monday nights some of us girls from high school hold a 'yack and yarn' in the library basement. We crochet and knit blankets for the hospital and talk. You should come."

I smiled, beginning to walk away. "I'll do my best to be there," I lied. My answer must have satisfied her because she waved and began pushing the stroller further down the block. I had no intention of hanging out with the girls from high school in the basement library. It might be fun, but the idea was depressing to me, like being trapped in the past. A magnet that keeps me from moving forward.

Picking up my pace, I walked to the end of the block and down Stony Avenue until I reached the corner Sadie was standing on. She was on her cell phone and didn't see me approaching. I thought I'd be really mean and jump on her shoulders to scare her, but I inadvertently overheard a sentence that piqued my curiosity. "No, I haven't told her yet. I will. I will. Okay, I'll see you later. Love you too," she said, her long shadow dancing with mine in the setting sun.

She pocketed the phone and jumped when she saw me out of the corner of her eye. "Jesus, Charli!" she said, holding her chest and taking a deep breath. "You scared me."

"Who were you talking to?" I asked nonchalantly, walking beside her.

Sadie's pale skin turned pink. "Oh, no one. My dad. Nothing."

She was acting weird, but I didn't have the energy to push her for more information. I was exhausted from the manual labor I'd put in that day and was looking forward to a sugary snack, a bucket of popcorn, and a movie to take me away from everything this town was throwing at me.

Like always, Sadie and I got bored halfway through the movie and started putting our own dialogue into the mouths of the actors. The Grand Marquee only played older movies, nothing from the past twenty years unless it was a cult classic or played into one of their Thursday night themes. The 1960 secret agent/super villain movie we chose did not hold our attention. We left in the middle of the movie, once the popcorn bucket was empty.

"Ice cream tacos?" I asked, despite how chilly the night had become. Something about walking down Main Street with Sadie made me nostalgic for our favorite treat.

"I love the way you think," Sadie commented, picking up her pace to make it to Froz T's. "How did I survive so long without you here?" she mused.

Laughing, I replied, "You probably weren't borderline diabetic then. I haven't had this much sugar since we were kids." I definitely had a boost of energy from the soda, licorice, and sugar coated gummy worms we'd devoured during the movie.

As we approached the entrance to Froz T's, I got excited that there wasn't a line out the door. Sadie's cell phone *pinged* as we walked into the warm building. She pulled it out of her back pocket, slowly following me to the counter as she read the text message she received. "Oh, Charli. I'm sorry. I have to go. Work stuff." She took a deep breath. It seemed like she wanted to say something else but decided against it.

"It's okay. Really." Maybe I didn't need more sugar anyway.

"I'll make it up to you. Coffee tomorrow morning at The Buzz?"

"And a chocolate croissant?" I asked, pushing my luck.

Sadie smiled warmly. "Honestly, Charli, is there any other way to have a coffee?"

Laughing, I followed her out the door and she cut

across the street, past Oakies' parking lot, to her apartment. I had too much sugar in me to go straight home, so I decided to walk through the Historic Downtown and loop through town circle where I caught a glimpse of the rising moon on the Whett River in the background.

As I walked down Sheridan, I realized I could stop in to check on Tammy under the guise of getting my box of books from her garage. Only, I didn't want to carry that box all the way back to the Alton House. Pulling out my phone, I texted Jake to see if he'd left the police station yet.

Jake: No. Could use an excuse to leave tho

Me: Meet me on the corner of Oak and Sheridan? U can help me carry a box of books home.

Jake: Lucky me

I laughed to myself at his comment. Since the road was muddy this morning, he would most likely have driven or ridden his bike, which was an easy solution.

When I reached Tammy's house, all the windows shone brightly, and they were were wide open despite the chill that had invaded the evening air. And it was quiet. Too quiet. Something was off, whether it was a bad vibe, or just someone in desperate need of a friend, I wasn't sure.

Walking up the front walk of the house, I couldn't shake this bad feeling. I stood in front of the door for a moment, biting my lip. It wouldn't hurt to just check in on her, right? To see if she needed anything? When I rang the doorbell, I realized I probably should have brought food or a plant or something that played into the illusion of wanting to help, rather than being nosy... or greedy for my box of books.

Tammy opened the storm door looking utterly

overwhelmed and exhausted. The hair that wasn't held back in a ponytail was frizzy and hovering in wisps around her head. She either wasn't wearing make up or the stress of her husband's arrest had aged her terribly. Her eyes were bloodshot and bags had grown like bruises beneath her eyes. Tammy leaned on the door for support as she greeted me. "Oh, hi Charli," she said through a sigh.

"Hi, Tammy, how are you doing?" I asked through the screen door.

"Oh, you know, holding up," she reported and sighed again.

I realized that James wasn't in her arms or screaming in the background. Maybe that was what was off. "James went to bed early, huh? You must be happy about that," I commented, trying not to obviously look past her and into the house.

Confusion covered Tammy's tired face. "Oh, no, I'm not that lucky." She laughed emptily. "He's next door at Allyson's. She offered to watch him while I pack up the house. Want to come in? It's getting chilly out there." Her shoulders wiggled, exaggerating the chill and she opened the screen door. "Did you come by for that box of books?" She yawned as I walked past her and into the foyer.

"Yes, in fact," I said, walking deeper into the living room; it wasn't much warmer inside. "I heard that you were thinking about moving out of town because of all of this," I shared, noticing how chaotic the house looked. Half-filled boxes sat on every surface. Piles of clothes, children's toys, and dishes sat in heaps on the floor. "I thought I'd come get it out of the way."

"Yeah, okay," she said, looking a bit dazed. Her eyes swept over the pile of junk on the dining room table and she added, "I just can't stay here. Too many bad memories. First Sara and the letters, now the murder and Jim's arrest." Tammy held her swollen belly and held in the tears. "It's just better to leave."

"I understand," I said, trying to be of some help.

"Besides, maybe now I can travel. I've always wanted to travel. I guess now I can." She leaned onto the back of a dining room chair.

I found it an odd thing to say, but Tammy looked so worn out and tired I don't think she knew she wasn't making much sense. "You have never traveled?"

She shook her head and began folding some of James' shirts that were sitting in a laundry basket on the high chair, absentmindedly. "No. Never. Always wanted to but Jim wouldn't allow it."

"Why not?" I asked, confused. I moved to take a seat but both the recliner and couch were covered in boxes and baskets full of unfolded laundry.

"He was too cheap. He never wanted to spend the extra dime," Tammy shared and put a pair of superhero-themed pajama pants down with an unexpected amount of force. Her voice edged with anger. "You know his idea of a vacation was camping in a tent on the outskirts of Libertyville? We had the opportunity to go to a cabin in Wisconsin last winter for free—I won a two night stay on a KLSX radio show—but he said it was a waste of gas." She sighed, fiddling with a pair of socks. "Didn't stop him from selling the reservations," she muttered. Her voice went back to worn-out exhaustion, "I guess now James and I can see the world."

Speechless, I stood beside the coffee table, soaking in the awkward silence. "Anyway, let me get that box for you," she said, waddling towards the kitchen.

"Oh, Tammy, let me," I insisted, walking towards her.

She put a hand up which stopped me in my tracks. "No, no. I can get it. The garage is in disarray thanks to the police. I shoved it aside—you'll never find it. I'll be right back."

I watched her waddle into the kitchen and heard the screen door slam as she walked into the backyard. Surveying the state of the house, *I* felt overwhelmed; I could only imagine how Tammy must feel. I thought I could help out by folding the laundry in the basket that Tammy was digging in earlier. There were piles of folded clothes on the dining room table, which sat on top of piles of papers and file folders.

Folding a dinosaur printed shirt, I threw it on the far end of the table where James' other shirts were piled. A piece of paper shot off the table and floated, slicing the air, until it hit the wooden floor. Squeezing my way between the table and china cabinet, I bent to pick it up. My Alton blood couldn't help but take a peek at it.

I had to look twice.

They were papers to sell Prescott's Grocers, dated a year ago.

CHAPTER 18

As I studied the paper, Tammy came waddling into the dining room holding the box of books over her belly. She placed them down on the hutch beside her with a grunt. "I didn't know you were looking to sell Prescott's," I said passively. I hadn't been in town for so long that there was probably a lot I didn't know. I was surprised that Mom or her gossip club didn't mention it as a tidbit during her gossip of this case.

"What?" Tammy asked, confused, as she turned around, stretching her back muscles. Her eyes traveled to the papers on the table in front of me. "Oh, uh, yeah," Tammy stumbled through her words, taking a step closer to the table. "We, uh, had a bit of a rough patch last year and thought we'd have to sell."

"Oh," I mused, confused. I must have gotten mixed messages; didn't Sadie say business was booming? "I thought I heard Jim was turning the business around with the Pineapple Bowl and stuff?"

Tammy shrugged, almost not paying attention to what I was saying. "You cold?" she asked suddenly, rubbing her arms. She began shutting the windows and closing the curtains, distracted. I guess that's what people called Pregnancy Brain. I couldn't blame her; there was so much going on in Tammy's life, her head must have been a jumbled mess.

"Just out of curiosity, what are you planning to do with the store now that you're leaving town and Jim is..." I couldn't finish the sentence. The news that he was the murderer was still a fresh wound in all of our minds.

"Well, the same interested party from a year ago put an offer in on the store. He contacted me this morning and I signed the papers this afternoon." Tammy moved to the living room as she talked, shutting windows and drawing curtains.

"Oh." Well, good for her. I moved to place the paper on the table, but was distracted by a Bill of Sale for the grocery store dated five days ago. *I wondered why she said it was sold this morning*, I thought to myself. *Pregnancy brain*, I decided.

Looking up to find a way through the mess of boxes, I saw Tammy's eyes look at me with pained regret. "You know, don't you?" she asked, standing under the subtle archway that separated the two rooms.

"Know what?" I asked. There was a lot I didn't know about this town anymore, apparently.

Tammy's arms were folded across her chest. "You saw the Bill of Sale, didn't you?" She moved towards me tentatively; each move measured, like a cat. She was surprising agile for being that far along in her pregnancy. Most woman with a belly that size waddled with exhaustion.

"Oh, Charli, I really did like you." She sighed. "Why did you have to be so nosy?"

It struck me then. She'd sold the store *before* Sara died. "Wait!" I exclaimed. "*You* did it?"

Disappointment dipped the corners of her lips. "Maybe you're not as smart as I assumed, but I can't let you go now. You'll ruin my plan." Her voice got firmer. "You're not going to ruin over a year of planning, Charli."

Stupefied over the news, I didn't notice Tammy grab the silver candelabra off the hutch, but I was able to put my arm up in time so that it connected with my shoulder instead of my head. Pain shot through my arm and I immediately stumbled over the clothes and dining room chairs to put as much distance as I could between Tammy and me.

Running into half-packed boxes and tripping over scattered belongings, I dashed to the front door to find it locked. I fumbled with the locks but had to jump out of the way when Tammy caught up to me. She was holding a box-cutter blade in her right hand now, and I knocked a plastic container of baby toys to the ground to form another obstacle between us. Tripping over a bouncing baby seat, she fell into the back of the arm chair. Horrified, I watched as she regained her balance with the orange box-cutter stabbing her swollen belly.

My first instinct was to help, but her maniacal laughter prevented me from moving forward; I froze trying to make sense of what was going on. She removed the letter opener and shook her belly with both hands. "It's not even real, Charli! Nothing in my marriage ever was," she admitted.

"But, but why? *How?*" I was dumbfounded. I don't think my brain had connected all the dots yet; it was still trying to figure out a way to escape, to survive.

She waved the blade of the box cutter wildly in the air as she talked. "Because no one would ever expect the eight-month pregnant wife as the murderer. After all, I was the one who set up the hunting trip that night, and I was the one who told Jim that Brian had canceled on him so he wouldn't have an alibi. I left James here that night and snuck into Prescott's." The surprised look on my face gave her glee. "Yes, I killed her! Did anyone ever suspect me? No." The next words she spoke through clenched teeth as if the reality of her plan was crumbling, "because it was part of the plan."

"Wait!" I exclaimed, holding up a hand and slowly moving backwards, careful not to trip. "You're not pregnant?"

Tammy rolled her eyes. "No, Charli. Catch up."

Backing up into the fireplace, I watched Tammy's moves. I could either dash to the front door or the kitchen from this spot.

Unexpectedly, Tammy began moving packed boxes from the wall until she found one that she wanted. "Honestly, Charli, you don't know what it's like to be in a relationship with someone who's never around. And when he is around, he doesn't pay attention to me." She stopped shifting through boxes and rolled her eyes dramatically. "And with an annoying child who won't shut up for three seconds. Jim never did anything but work. No vacations," she said sardonically, dropping a box to the ground. "No dinners outside the house." She dropped another box, its thump loud and menacing. Then she paused and asked, "Do you know the last time I had a day to myself? A trip to Sheridan for a haircut or a new outfit? A new pair of clothes? No, we bought everything, *everything*, second-hand. Nothing new was ever good enough for me. It was never about me or my wants. So I did something about it... and I was going to take Jim down too." Anger shot through her, rattling her mussed hair. "The things he thought I didn't know he did with that girl!" she said, disgusted.

Tammy began moving boxes again. "It wasn't hard to kill Sara, you know. I kinda enjoyed scaring the crap out of her that night. She was always such a brat; walking around like her poop didn't stink, like she knew she had Jim wrapped around her pinky and acting like it was all a smug little secret from me." She opened a box and shifted it around. "I knew it was the perfect motive for murder. This way both of them paid."

Deciding that that wasn't the box she wanted, she shoved it aside, letting its contents spill onto the floor. She laughed then, before grabbing another box. "Why do you think I invited you into the garage? So you could see the murder weapon out there in the open! It was only a matter of time before you overheard something at the police station and pieced it together. Oh, don't look so innocent," she said, scolding me. My eyes once again darted from her, to the front door, to the kitchen, and back again. "Everyone knows your mother is the queen of gossip in this town and ever since you came back, you've spent nearly all your time with that deputy," she said, matter-of-factly.

Tammy opened another box and shifted around its contents. "You were a perfect pawn in my game. Now," she said, taking out a small package from the box and revealing a handgun. "Do you want to do this the easy way or the hard way?" she asked, putting in the bullets and pointing it at me.

CHAPTER 19

My heart raced. My body was no longer chilled, but warm with adrenaline. Only one small move and I could be a goner. It wasn't the threat of death that scared me, but the pain I'd feel before it. *Stall*, was the only thing I could think to do as my eyes once again slid over the locks on the front door.

"What?" I said, putting up my hands. "How do you think you'll get away with my murder?" I asked. My frantic mind was also curious about this little glitch.

"Easy," Tammy said, waving the gun. "There was a stranger lurking in my garage so I shot 'em. I'll cry a good tear when it turned out only to be that nosy Charli Parker getting that box of books I'd promised her." Tammy was in front of me now, the gun only a few feet from my head. "So, let's take that walk." She nudged her head towards the back of the house.

It was a good story. I knew no one would think anything foul from poor, pregnant, grief-stricken Tammy.

With one last effort for my safety, I blindly tried to grab a weapon from behind me. My fist settled for the iron handle of the fireplace poker. I whipped it forward to knock her hand—the barrel of the gun—from my face. My body twitched when the loud crack of the gun went off, shattering part of the plaster ceiling above us.

No longer afraid of hurting a pregnant lady, I threw my body forward, knocking Tammy to the ground and the gun went skidding across the wooden floor towards the bedroom. On top of the padded mound of her fake pregnancy, I tried to restrain Tammy so I could safely get away. But, dang, she was strong.

I struggled to hold onto her hands, but she kept slipping them out of my grasp; it was like trying to hold onto a fish. This was starting to become a losing battle.

It wasn't the stab of the metal scissors in my back that caught my attention at first, it was how still she had become. Her red-rimmed eyes hungrily studied me for a reaction and then the searing pain shot out from my shoulder blade.

Arching my body and yelling out in pain, Tammy removed the bloody scissors from my back and pushed me off of her. I held my arm and moaned in agony, unable to focus on what might happen in the next sixty seconds because the pain was too great.

"You're going to do this the hard way, aren't you?" she asked, climbing on top of me and holding the open pair of scissors to my throat. The pressure my wound was undergoing was unspeakable. My eyes began to water from the pain and from the realization that tonight I just might die. I watched her through blurry vision as I bit my bottom lip to prevent from blubbering.

A loud boom filled the room and I winced. Urging myself to open my eyes again, I saw Jake at the front door in his uniform, pointing a gun at Tammy who was still straddling me with a pair of bloody scissors to my throat.

"Put the scissors down, Tammy," he said, his voice forceful and persuasive.

After several long seconds of Tammy's eyes darting between my throat and Jake's pistol, she slowly stood up. Her hands were in the air, still gripping the pair of bloody scissors. She turned away from me to face Jake. "Drop the scissors," Jake demanded once more.

The metal utensils clashed onto the wooden floor

beside my head, and I tried to take a deep breath when I noticed I was nearly hyperventilating. "You okay, Charli?" Jake asked, not taking his eyes from Tammy.

I moaned and grabbed my shoulder as Jake came closer and kicked the scissors out of Tammy's reach. Honestly, I never thought I'd be one of *those* people in this type of situation: a blubbering baby. But I think this stab in the back—no pun intended—was the last straw. The painful realization that my marriage was over, the emotional move back to Alton Oaks, and being surrounded by the people who never stopped loving me, sent me to tears (and maybe gave way to some restrained rage for the time I'd lost). It all came pouring out as I struggled to sit up, feeling warm, sticky blood soak through my shirt and sweater.

"On your knees!" Jake's voice was angrier this time.

Tammy suddenly lowered her hands, grabbed her swollen stomach and dramatically cried out, "Oh! The baby!"

Too quickly, she distracted Jake with her cries and slapped away his gun. She grabbed his legs, sending him backwards onto a heap of cleaning products. Almost reflexively, she climbed on top of him and savagely wrung her hands around his neck.

Seeing Jake on the floor and Tammy once again about to hurt someone, I swallowed my wails. Without too much thought, I grabbed the candelabra from underneath the dining room table beside me. It was the same one Tammy had hit me with earlier and I enjoyed the irony in the situation. That restrained emotional rage broke through its barriers and gave me the adrenaline to forget about the torment in my shoulder, spring off the floor, and smack her across the back of the head with a grunt. The *thwack* it made was strangely satisfying.

Stun drenched Jake's face as she slumped to the

side. He quickly pushed Tammy's body off of him and restrained her in a pair of handcuffs as she remained unconscious.

"Are you all right?" Jake asked, a hand on my bloody shoulder.

Woozy with pain and the loss of the pain-killing adrenaline, I fell to my knees.

CHAPTER 20

When I opened my eyes, I was in a sterile, muted, yellow room with beeping sounds out of eyesight. My eyelids were heavy and itchy, my mouth felt like a cotton ball.

"Hey, Charli May," Alex said as I looked to my right. He looked down at me over a clipboard, through his wire-rimmed glasses. His hair was characteristically out of place, in every direction. "You know," he said, putting down the clipboard in the holder at the foot of the bed, and pouring me a glass of water, "if you wanted to spend more time with me, we could have just gone to Oakies. You didn't have to almost get murdered."

I laughed and it hurt. I drained the cup of water Alex had handed to me and responded, "Well, I thought I'd go for something more theatrical."

Alex rolled his eyes. "Don't turn into another Bailey," he said in a hushed tone, taking the glass from me and putting it back on the bedside table.

Trying to sit up, I winced at the pain in my shoulder. "You'll be fine," Alex said, fiddling with the instruments on the side of the bed. "You were just stabbed is all."

"Oh, is that all?" I asked jokingly.

Alex looked from the instruments to me and said, "Mom's on the way, so I just upped your pain meds."

"Best. Brother. Ever," I said as I found the button that made the bed rise so I could sit up. "I bet she's having a field day."

Alex looked me dead in the eye and said, "Oh, you have *no* idea. She can't wait to hear the firsthand account."

I groaned. I felt obligated to share the story with her ever since I'd kept that key detail that I was the one who'd tipped off the police about the knife in Jim's garage from her. Only, I really didn't feel up to her questions at this moment. "I don't suppose you could get me out of this?" I asked. "Maybe bloody up my gown a bit, put a bandage over my head? Hey, can't you medically induce a coma?" Maybe if I looked worse, she would be preoccupied with my life rather than the gossip.

Alex laughed and shook his head. "You have nothing to worry about, Charli," he said. After glancing at his watch, he added, "I need to go finish my rounds, but Sadie will be around soon. She has popped in and out from the pediatrics ward ever since you were admitted."

"Good. She'll be a good buffer when Mom gets here," I said, already starting to feel the pain killers kick in.

Alex laughed and moved toward the door. Before leaving, he turned to me and said, "Glad you're okay, Charli May."

I smiled, letting my body relax from the medicine. I realized that my bangs weren't in my face anymore and touched my hand to my head—inadvertently tugging on the IV in my arm and cursed. Someone had pinned my bangs back with a bobby pin and I liked it. It was a simple fix to finally see things more clearly.

Closing my eyes, I let my muscles loosen and felt the drugs eat away at the pain until it disappeared. I let the beeping machines try to carry me away to sleep, feeling like I could dance my way out the hospital doors, if I wanted.

A knock at the door made my eyes open much more slowly than I'd anticipated. Jake, dressed in off-duty clothes, poked his head in with a handful of small white flowers wrapped in cellophane. "Charli?" he said tentatively.

"That's me," I said, a bit too enthusiastically and raised my hands. The IV got caught on the bedrail again and I cursed. The medicine definitely ate away at my common sense as well as the pain. "Hey, remember that time we fought off a crazy, faux-pregnant, murder lady? Memories," I remarked, letting my head bounce back into the cushioned pillow behind me.

Jake laughed and walked further into the room. "You up for a visitor?"

Concern draped across my face, playfully. "Why? Is my mother with you?"

He laughed and walked to the bed, placing the flowers on the table. "No, no. Just me."

"Good," I said losing my ability to control the filter on my words. "'Cause she's gonna kiiiiiillll me." I exaggerated the word for emphasis.

"Listen," Jake started, sitting sideways on the bed, "I just wanted to thank you for your help out there in the field. I never should have let her surprise me like that. I'm sorry."

I waved my hand and nestled my head deeper into the pillow. "'S nothing. We're even. Girl nearly cut my head clean off." I slid my finger across my neck to emphasize, "I got your six," I said, pounding my chest twice with my fist to sound tough. "I used that word right, right?" I asked.

Jake nodded, finding humor in my actions.

Then my face turned stone still. "Oh, my gosh. My mother's gonna kill me, Jake. Cause I almost got killed; she's gonna kill me." My head felt heavy suddenly. "She's mad 'cause I din' tell her about the knife in the garage like I tol' you. Why shou' I tell her?" I asked, slurring my words with exhaustion. Then once again, with dramatic concern, I pointed out, "She's gonna kill me, Jake!"

I had definitely lost control of any filters I had. Jake smiled at the nonsense coming out of my mouth. "No she won't; I won't let her."

"Good. She'll lis'en to a policeman," I said, closing my eyes a little longer each time I blinked.

"I'm real glad you came back home, Charli," Jake said. "I hope you stay."

"Me too," I replied. I opened my eyes to add, "'cept, you know, the whole stabbing-killy thing."

Smiling, Jake said, "Yeah, except that part." He put the flowers on the table where a pink plastic water pitcher sat. "Your hair is different," he pointed out.

"I blame Sadie," I said, feeling my breathing get slower.

"I like it," he admitted with trepidation. "I don't remember your eyes being so green. They're kinda like a meadow in a fog or a storm or something."

I laughed half-heartedly, thinking he was making a joke.

"Knock, knock!" Sadie's voice drifted in before her. I felt Jake's weight disappear from the mattress beside me and I opened my eyes. Sadie walked into the room in her sea green, cartoon-printed scrubs and a Froz T's bag in her arms. "Oh, hey, Jake," she said, passing him and putting the bag on the table, next to his flowers.

"Sorry to interrupt," she started, grabbing my wrist and looking at her wristwatch to take my pulse. After a few moments, she dropped my wrist and continued talking. "Of course, you'd wake up the second I walked into my apartment, Charli. When Alex texted me and said you were up, I jumped back into my truck, got some ice cream tacos, and drove straight back here.

Passed your mom on the way, she was biking past the Miller's farm—really huffing it, so you have about ten minutes before she gets here."

Sadie looked at the chart at my bed and smiled. "Looks like you'll be passed out by then. Alex made sure of that."

"I'll get going," Jake said, waving and putting his hands in his pockets. "Nice seeing you again, Sadie," he said and then turned to me and added, "Thanks again, Charli," and walked out.

Putting the chart down, Sadie moved back beside me and pulled out two clear plastic containers filled with vanilla ice cream tacos, topped with brownie bites, colorful sprinkles, and drizzled in caramel and marshmallow sauce. She whispered, "Don't tell anyone I brought these," and winked. "I even splurged for the make-your-own tacos," she added.

Sitting on the edge of my bed, she grabbed her taco and began to munch. I, on the other hand, was having difficulty finding the energy (or the appetite) to eat mine. "I love 'scream tacos, Sadie," I said, slurring my words because I was too tired to form them. "But meso tired."

Sadie put her half-eaten taco back in its case and looked at me indecisively. "Charli?" she asked for my attention hesitantly.

"Hm?" I asked, finding it a struggle to open my eyes again.

She squirmed a little then grabbed my hand and said, "I need to tell you something very important. I've been scared to tell you... but I'm going to take advantage of your medically induced stupor." There was a long pause before she spoke again—the beeping of the machines nearly put me to sleep, but I managed to open my eyes briefly when she started talking once more.

"You know, you've been gone a long time... and I

know your relationship with Alex has been strained. But he works here, and I work here, and we live three houses from each other, and we grew up together and... and so it's almost impossible for..." She paused and took a deep breath, squeezing my hand. Through the slits of my eyes I saw her pained expression as she blew her auburn hair out of her face. "Well, Alex and I have been seeing each other for about ten months now."

The next few sentences shot out of her mouth like aimless bullets and I felt her body tense as she gripped my hand tighter. "Don't be mad. I've wanted to tell you. But I wanted to tell you in person, but you didn't come home for Christmas. And then you moved back, and we were dealing with Jackson, and then Sara's murder, and work... and I'm *so* happy, Charli," she said, wrapping both of her cold hands around mine. "Please don't be mad."

With all the strength I had left, I squeezed her hand weakly and smiled. "My two fa'rit people. Me so like dis," I said and pulled the sheets up to my shoulders. "Sleep now. Night-night."

And as the pain killers lulled me to sleep, I heard Sadie gather up any evidence of Froz T's and walk towards the door. Sleep stole me away just as I heard my mother's voice in the doorway.

Perfect timing.

CHAPTER 21

The next morning I was discharged from the hospital, my arm in a sling and prescribed a bottle of pain killers. Since my parents didn't have a car, and Alex had advised Mom against using Mrs. Kratsky's golf cart, Sadie graciously offered to drive me home from the hospital.

It was a warm day and I didn't need the sweater Sadie let me borrow. She brought me an old t-shirt of hers to wear home since mine was covered in blood. Being as short as she was, her shirt just met the band of my jeans and it made me incredibly uncomfortable. I kept tugging down at it and adjusting my sling.

Without the use of my left arm, it was a lot harder to haul myself into her big black truck. It might have been the pain killers, but I was laughing at the show we must have put on to anyone who was watching. Luckily, a paramedic nearby took pity on us and helped hoist me in by my hips.

When we were both finally inside the truck, and Sadie had helped buckle me in, she reported, "Well, I was going to ask if you wanted to stop for a bite to eat before I took you to your mom's, but I don't know if I'd get you back into the car."

My stomach suddenly rumbled with hunger at the thought of food. In response, Sadie said, "How about I bring you a big ol' burrito plate from Oakies?"

"That would be amazing," I said, putting a hand on my stomach to quiet it down. "And a plate of s'more nachos from Froz Ts?"

Sadie rolled her eyes. "Well, obviously." Then added, "And loaded cookie fries." I could almost taste the wedges of gooey chocolate chip cookies covered in chocolate sauce, and sprinkled with peanut butter and butterscotch chips.

My stomach groaned again and I rubbed it to quiet it down. "That sounds utterly perfect," I replied, licking my lips.

The radio played quietly in the background as Sadie navigated through the parking lot and back onto Oak Street. Farmland still stood between the hospital and the town. I watched the tractors work the soil and the pain killers kept my body relaxed.

"So," Sadie began, hesitantly testing the waters. "Do you remember anything about yesterday? More specifically, my visit?"

Her voice quavered a bit with nervousness. A lot of my thoughts from yesterday were hazy. "I remember you owe me an ice cream taco," I said, turning my head to face her. "A build-your-own taco with rainbow sprinkles and brownie bites. You can't tell me I dreamed that," I added.

She sat and gripped the steering wheel tensely. I knew my evasiveness was killing her. She was quiet as we rolled out of the farmland and into the town where the speed limit made us come to a crawl.

"Oh, I'm just playing you," I said, nudging her in the arm and then winced when the movement resulted in pain.

She looked over at me with a tentative smile. "I think you are perfect for each other," I added, looking out the window at the influx of people as we approached Main Street.

Relief spread across Sadie's smile as she glanced at me. "For real? You're not just saying that?"

I nodded. "My two favorite Alton Oakians together?

That's darn near perfect."

Sadie let out a huge sigh of relief. "Thanks, Charli," she said and dropped one hand from the steering wheel; her body instantly melting away any tension.

I gave her a reassuring smile and watched the scenery melt into a more rural scene as we went past the junior high school. Mr. K. was in his driveway, on one knee, pumping air into a child's bicycle and waved as we drove by. "You know," I started with a sigh, "it was only seven days ago when I called you up and said I was coming back home?"

Sadie nodded. "Seems like ages ago," she said. We waved to Mrs. Kratsky who passed us in her golf cart. She responded with her *hee-haw, hee-haw* horn. "Do you have any regrets about coming back here?" she asked.

Looking out the windshield, I saw the Alton House come into view in the distance. As we drove past Jake's and Rip's houses, I thought about Sadie's question. "No," I said, then I shot her a sly smile and added, "Well, not right now, at least."

She understood the undertone and said, "I'm *so* glad you're back, Charli."

We drove past Bailey and Jenna's houses and I saw the Alton House clearly. It might be big and historic, but it was broken. People thought the house was a well-kept classy museum on the inside, so well put together from a distance, but I knew the interior. It wasn't always fun living in it, but it was home.

"Me too, Sadie," I replied as she pulled onto the long dirt driveway. The wheels crunched across the gravel and the smell of musty wood and fresh cut grass filled the air. "I've missed coming home."

THE END

ABOUT THE AUTHOR

Megan Rivers is a former world adventurer and life-long writer who graduated from Northern Michigan University with a degree in writing and literature. She recently returned to live in her hometown of Evergreen Park, Illinois, with her spoiled pup Gracie. She teaches outdoor and environmental education. When not writing, she loves to visit thrift stores, bask in the outdoors, get lost in a good book, or cook delectable vegan dishes.